MADBALL

FREDRIC BROWN

Black Gat Books • Eureka, California

MADBALL

Published by Black Gat Books
A division of Stark House Press
1315 H Street
Eureka, CA 95501, USA
griffinskye3@sbcglobal.net
www.starkhousepress.com

MADBALL
Originally published 1953 in paperback by Dell Books, New York, copyright ©
1953 by Fredric Brown; reprinted 1961 by Gold Medal Books, Greenwich,
copyright © 1961 by Fredric Brown. A condensed version edited by the author
was published under the title "The Pickled Punks" in *The Saint Detective
Magazine*, June-July 1953.

ISBN-13: 978-1-944520-74-8

Book design by Jeff Vorzimmer, ¡caliente!design, Austin, Texas
Cover art from the original Dell edition by Griffith Foxley

First Stark House Press/Black Gat Edition: June 2019

FIRST EDITION

CHAPTER ONE

Mack Irby stood leaning on a heavy cane listening to the grind of the talker for the unborn show. The carnival crowd streaming down the midway flowed around him. There was ironical amusement on his lean face as he listened. Mystery of Sex read the banner over the front.

"Here it is, boys, the show they been talking about, the show you came out here to see, this is it, the sex mystery exposed, here's where you see it, male and female, male and female naked and unadorned, here's where you see everything, I mean everything, right before your very eyes, the naked truth, all on the inside and all for one thin dime, one dime ten cents the whole show, the mystery of sex, doctors and nurses admitted free, scientific and you see it all for one dime, now going on . . ."

Burt had done all right by himself, Mack Irby thought, in finding a new talker. The guy was okay. There were a few phrases that Mack would have used himself if he'd have thought of them. Not that it mattered now, not that he'd ever have to grind again for an unborn show or any other kind of show.

Mack Irby limped only a little as he made his way to the front of the ticket box. The talker reached to tear a ticket off the roll and then stopped as he saw Irby grinning at him. "How are the pickled punks?" Irby asked him.

He got an answering if slightly puzzled grin. "You with it?" the talker asked.

The talker was a little guy, sharp eyed, sharp nosed, but with a good voice, a voice that proved he'd done spieling back before p.a. systems mechanized it. Irby said, "Just got back. How go things?"

"Pretty fair. Say—" The talker looked down and apparently noticed the cane. "You the guy who did the grinding here before? Uh . . . Kirby?"

"Irby. Mack Irby. Yeah."

"Glad to know you, Mack. I'm Barney King." He reached down over the ledge to shake hands. "Stick around. Burt'll be closing up pretty soon and we can have a drink."

Irby pulled a flat pint out of his hip pocket and handed it up. "Have the drink now, I got a dame to look up."

Barney King tilted the bottle and drank, his Adam's apple bobbing like a cork. "Good stuff," he said, glancing at the label before he passed it back. "Thanks."

"How's Burt? Cranky as ever?"

"We get along. Go on in and say hi to him."

Irby started in, then hesitated. "Any marks in there?"

"A few. Half a dozen, maybe."

He didn't want to see Burt anyway, not tonight. He'd never really liked Burt. All right to work for and a damn good pitchman, but pretty dull company.

He took out cigarettes, offered the talker one.

"Then I might queer his pitch on the sex books. But you can tell Burt I'm back and I'll look him up tomorrow. I'll be around a few days anyhow."

"Not going to ride out the season? Listen, you can tie up, easy. The model show needs a talker; Johnny Dane took off early and headed south. Slim's been doing his own talking but he'd be damn glad to get you."

"Nah, only two weeks left. I'd just as soon loaf it out, have myself some fun after that goddam hospital. And I got my stake."

"Burt said you got some moolah out of the accident."

"Two grand—not bad for seven weeks. And with what I had stashed up to then I'm okay and nuts to taking a job for just two weeks. I was lucky."

"The guy in the car with you was killed, wasn't he?"

"Yeah, Charlie Flack. You here the seven weeks?"

"Six of 'em," Barney King said. "First guy Burt tried turned out to be a lush. Say, I better grind a while or Burt'll be out here to see what happened to me."

"Okay, Barney. So long."

"Here it is, boys, hurry, hurry, hurry, the show you came out to see, the mystery of sex, the naked truth, male and female unadorned and only one thin dime . . ." Mack Irby walked on down the midway and despite the limp and the cane he walked on air. He told himself, This is it, boy, this is the show you been waiting for. Continuous and stay as long as you like and all for forty-two thousand bucks. Safely waiting to be picked up.

And almost three thousand more in honest money, the nine hundred and fifty he'd stashed in postal savings during the season up to the time of the accident, and the two thousand he'd got from the insurance company.

It needed music, that walk down the bright midway, "Hail the Conquering Hero Comes." The merry-go-round was playing "Dardanella" instead, but that didn't matter really. The music Mack Irby heard wasn't the merry-go-round's organ nor the three-piece combo of the jig show; it was the overall sound of the carnival on a busy night, voices and laughter and the strident selling spieling grinding over p.a. systems and the crack of rifles in the shooting gallery and singing yelling shuffling, the thud of baseballs and the soft ratchets of fortune wheels and the bassdrum call to bally, try your luck, mister, pitch till you win, the big show just about to start, a few seats left, three balls for a dime, see the strangest people on earth, win a kewpie doll for the little woman, get 'em while they're hot, pick your lucky number, and inside the little lady will show you, hurry, hurry, win an Armour ham, see the alligator boy, this is the show you came to see, naked and unadorned, every number wins a prize, the show's about to start, step right up, try your luck . . .

Mack Irby walking down the midway, a rich man now.

God, what a break that accident had been. It had meant the whole forty-two thousand was his, instead of only a third of it. Charlie Flack had been tough about that two-thirds split—but with some justification, Irby had to admit. It was Charlie who knew the ropes on robbing banks, Charlie who'd cased the job, who'd done the brainwork and given the orders. He, Irby, had been green at anything bigger than petty larceny. Yes, Charlie had really earned that two-thirds split, if he'd lived to take it.

Charlie had been a careful guy. Mack Irby remembered how carefully Charlie had felt him out and then tested him before he'd chosen him as a partner for a job, how careful Charlie had been in planning every little detail in advance, even to how they'd stash the loot and not touch it till the end of the season. Charlie had even been a careful driver; that accident the next night after the robbery hadn't been Charlie's fault at all. He'd talked Charlie into driving over to a roadhouse he knew near Glenrock for a little private celebration but they were on their way there when it happened and neither of them had even had a drink as yet. The other driver had been drunk and speeding and had been on the wrong side of the road. And a cop car had seen it happen; that's why there hadn't been any doubt about responsibility and why the insurance company that carried liability for the other guy had settled like a shot.

Of course a broken leg and seven weeks in the hospital hadn't been fun, but what wonderful news it had been when they'd told him Charlie Flack was dead. Only he and Charlie had known where the bank loot was hidden and now only he knew, and it was all his, three-thirds of that beautiful hunk of moolah.

And maybe he'd inherit Charlie's girl, too. He'd know about that pretty soon now.

Unless someone had snagged off Maybelle already ... He saw he was about to pass the mitt camp, the little square top with the big palms—human palms, not potted ones—on banners on each side of the entrance, and the bigger banner across the top. Dr.

Magus, it read, Palmistry, Astrology, Card and Crystal Readings. Walk In.

Mack Irby stopped. Right here and now, if Doc wasn't busy, he could find out what the score was on Maybelle. If she'd tied up with somebody else it would be smarter not to look her up. Making a pass could cause trouble, and trouble was the last thing he wanted to risk now.

He stepped close to the entrance. "Doc," he called. Dr. Magus stepped into the entrance. A little man with a gray goatee, silvery hair, sharp eyes twinkling behind gold-rimmed glasses, dapper.

He held out his hand. "Mack. Good to see you. No biz, and I was getting set to knock off and drown my sorrows. Come on in and have a drink with me."

"Just wanted to ask you a question, Doc. Afraid I haven't got time for a drink, want to catch somebody before they get away."

Dr. Magus smiled. "You have plenty of time, my boy. The model show is still putting on a bally—I can hear them—and that means there's at least one more show."

"You win, doc." Irby chuckled. "One drink."

He followed Dr. Magus inside.

"We'll even use glasses," Dr. Magus said. He poured them each a drink into a Lily cup. "So we can make it a toast to your getting back. Luck, Mack."

"Thanks, Doc." They drank. "How've things been going on the lot?"

"Fine. And now I'll save you asking that question. Maybelle is still free."

Mack Irby stared at him. How the hell had Doc known he'd wanted to ask about Maybelle? The guess that he'd been heading for the model show wouldn't have been a hard one for him to make, under the circumstances. Just back from seven weeks in a hospital. But there were three girls with the model show and either of the other two besides Maybelle would have been a more natural guess for Doc. Trixie Connor because she put out for cash and, unless she'd already made a date, she'd be a sure thing. Or Honey McGlassen because he'd had fun with her before, nothing steady but half a dozen times maybe. And he'd never once made a pass at Maybelle because Maybelle had been Charlie Flack's woman.

Suddenly a frightening thought hit Mack Irby. What if Doc, that smart little bastard of a mentalist, really could read minds? What if right now he was reading about—he tried to jerk his mind away from the bank robbery, from the money and where the money was hidden. Don't think about—

He said quickly, "Thanks, Doc. But I really got to run. Got to see someone else before I look up Maybelle." He got out of there as fast as he could. Still worrying. He'd make a point of giving Doc as wide a berth as possible while he was still here at the carney.

Then he started thinking about Maybelle, and the fact that she was still free, and that was enough to get his mind off Doc. He'd had a yen for Maybelle all season but he hadn't dared show it while Charlie was still alive.

The merry-go-round lay ahead, with its mirror-sided ticket booth. He turned a little off course to walk straight toward one of the mirrors, to take a look at himself. Not bad, he thought. Not even with a slight limp and a cane.

Good build, broad shoulders. Maybe not as broad as Charlie's had been, but then his face made up for that. It was a lean, hard, handsome face, a face women liked.

His suit looked all right, too, cleaned and freshly pressed, and the solid color lemon yellow tie went beautifully with the dark blue shirt. He grinned at himself and his reflection grinned back, showing yellowish, irregular teeth that stopped the grin; well, now that he had all the money in the world he'd have those teeth cleaned and straightened. Ought to have had it done long ago. He straightened his tie, walked around the ticket booth and on down the midway.

Down the row of hanky panks—the string game, the fish pond, the fortune wheel, the milk bottle game—and there weren't any marks in front of the milk bottle game so he stopped there. Reminded. He'd need a place to take Maybelle tonight, if he got her, and he might as well line it up now. It wouldn't go to waste. If he couldn't get Maybelle he'd find someone else; after seven weeks' continence he wasn't sleeping alone tonight. And Jesse Rau, who ran the ball game, pitched a sleeping top he was always willing to rent for an hour or for a night. Ordinarily Jesse and his punk, Sammy the halfwit, slept in it, but if he rented it for all night he and the punk would doss down under one of the bally platforms.

Mack said, "Hi, Jess. Got your top rented tonight?"

"Glad you're back with us, Mack. Just get in?"

"Yeah. How about the top?"

"I dunno. It's cool tonight and—"

Irby said, "Five bucks?" He didn't want to argue. Jesse usually got two or three bucks. He put the five on the ledge, knowing Jesse would take it. And what the hell was five bucks, tonight?

As he walked away he heard Jesse telling Sammy to get their stuff out of the top.

The music from the jig show passed him, and the grind Joe Linder was doing for the freak show and then he was standing at the back of the tip in front of the model show. Two of the girls were out for the bally, Honey and Maybelle, standing there in thin silk kimonas that showed every curve of their bodies, and as he looked at Maybelle's body he felt himself breathing a little hard, almost feeling dizzy he wanted her so bad.

He raised his hand on the chance that she'd notice the movement and see him, and miraculously she did. With a finger of the raised hand he made a little circular pointing gesture that meant around behind the top and caught her slight nod.

He went around back and took a slug, a big slug, out of the pint bottle while he waited. It emptied the bottle; he'd have to remember to get another one.

Then the canvas lifted and Maybelle ducked under it.

His arms were around her almost before she could straighten up, pulling her against him, his hands running down the silk of her back, down over her buttocks cupping them, pulling her so tightly against him that they were almost off balance.

"Maybelle honey, I got Jesse's top for tonight. Will you come there after the show?"

Her voice, low, throaty, sounded amused. "You sure don't waste time, do you, Mack?"

"Honey, you know I been hot for you all season. Only on account of my being a friend of Charlie's—"

She fended off his lips. "Now, now, don't mess my make-up or I won't."

"How soon can you be there?"

"Hour maybe. Midnight or a little after." She shook her head in mock bewilderment. "You act like a man who hasn't had a woman in seven weeks. Didn't you even make a quick stop on the way here?"

His quick breath told her without words that he hadn't; She laughed a little. Then, God help him, with him holding her as he was she did a grind.

Then she suddenly pushed him away and went back under the canvas sidewall. He had to concentrate a moment on standing straight without falling.

He got control back and laughed a little at himself. What a woman. Forty-two grand and a dame like that. He'd take her with him when he left here in a few days, take her to Florida for the winter, or maybe Mexico City; they'd have fancy hotel suites instead of tiny sleeping tops, suites with oversize beds and silk sheets and mirrored ceilings. But tonight the sleeping top would do.

He walked around the tops behind the midway to Pop Wilson's trailer to buy another pint and from there right to Jesse's sleeping top to wait for her.

He lay there waiting, sweating a little despite the coolness, thinking, What if she doesn't come, and then thinking, If she doesn't after doing that to me I'll kill her.

But she came, and the first time was fierce and fast, almost an explosion, but the second time was wonderful, and the third, and between them he lay naked and sweating and panting in the cool air. A foolish thing to do and a hell of a good way to catch pneumonia. But that doesn't matter if you're not going to live till morning.

CHAPTER TWO

The murderer, after he straightened up from bending over the body, stood completely still for a long moment, there in the shadow. The thud of that tent stake had been so loud that it seemed impossible that no one had heard it. But there was no sound, no movement.

Cautiously now and keeping to the shadow of the sidewall he walked around the penny arcade top to the midway and stood there ready to step out into the light but listening first for footsteps, not wanting to stick his head out to look around. No sound, and he took the step.

And saw Dolly Quintana coming toward him. Wearing moccasins; that accounted for his not having heard her. She stopped and stared at him and the direction of her gaze and now the kinetic sense of something round and heavy in his hand told him the horrible blunder he'd made. In being so quiet, in concentrating so hard on walking softly, he'd forgotten to drop the weapon he'd just killed Mack Irby with.

It was almost a fatal mistake. For just a fraction of a second he thought that it would be fatal, fatal for Dolly, that he'd have to kill her with it too because she'd seen it. Then he realized she had stopped, still three paces away, that no matter how fast he moved she'd have time at least to scream, possibly even to turn and run, too. And a scream would bring people running even at half past two in the morning.

So he turned and tossed the tent stake back the way he'd come, casually as though it was nothing important. And casually too he said, "Hi, Dolly. Know if the chow top is still open?"

"I hope so." She came forward again now. "Couldn't get to sleep and I'm hungry. I'm going for a hamburger." He fell in beside her. "I can use a cup of coffee myself." His mind worked furiously. This was dynamite. Dolly was the wife—or woman, it didn't matter—of Leon Quintana, the knife thrower with the freak show, and Quintana was insanely, murderously jealous. It was dangerous just to walk or talk with Dolly; yet now he had to stay with her until he had a chance to kill her without her being able to scream. Or until he figured another answer. It didn't matter right now that she'd seen him with that stake but tomorrow—or for that matter any time now—when Mack Irby was found dead back there, killed with a stake and near where Dolly had seen him, Dolly had his number, in spades.

He wondered if he was strong enough and quick enough to choke her to death without her being able to scream, here and now, beside her. He glanced sidewise at her, at her neck, thinking the move out, weighing the chances of being able to do it silently. Then he heard the shuffle of footsteps and saw that Jesse Rau had just come out of the freak show top, where he must have been sleeping after renting his own sleeping top to Mack Irby, heading for the doniker. By the time he was out of sight they were too near the still-lighted chow top and the chance to silence Dolly the simple way was gone.

He spoke quickly under his breath. "We better not go in together, Dolly. But I want to tell you something. You go in first, take a table away from anyone else."

He saw her slight nod and stopped long enough to let her go in alone. When he entered a minute later he saw to his relief that the place was almost empty. Aside from Dolly at a table way back, Barney King was the only other customer and he was sitting at the counter. He said hi to Barney and then went back and sat down at a table next to Dolly's but not even facing her. He faced, though, so he could watch the entrance and could also keep an eye on Barney and on Hank, who was now waddling over to take their orders. When Hank had gone away again and was out of earshot back of the counter, he said, just loudly enough so Dolly could hear but his voice wouldn't reach Barney or Hank, "Don't look toward me, Dolly, but listen. I'm going to reach over and drop something in your lap. Look at it, but look under the edge of the table."

He made sure both Barney and Hank still had their backs toward him, took a quick look at the entrance, and then stood up and leaned across far enough to toss into Dolly's lap the tight roll of bills, still with the rubber band around it just as he'd taken it from Irby's pocket. He hadn't even counted it, but it had looked like several hundred dollars.

Watching the entrance again he heard the faint sound of the rubber band and then a gasp from Dolly. Her voice was a whisper. "What's this for?"

"Count it and I'll tell you."

Counting it would clear up any misapprehension Dolly might have about what he was trying to buy, at any rate, and he was curious himself to know just how much he'd given her. He took a quick glance at her to be sure she was counting it below the edge of the table; she was.

She looked up at him, her eyes wide. "Two hundred and forty. What in hell—"

"Shhh, put it away quick. And don't look at me."

"But what's it for?"

"For forgetting you saw me on the midway tonight— and especially what I had in my hand."

"But—oh!"

The oh showed she'd just remembered what he'd been holding when he'd stepped out in front of her, and that she guessed now what he must have used it for.

Hank was coming over with their orders, a hamburger and coffee for Dolly and coffee for him, bringing them both at once to save a trip. He collected from each of them and then went back.

Then, "A deal?" he asked Dolly quietly.

Her voice was low, almost a whisper, but it sounded hard. "Damn right it's a deal. And I don't care who you killed back there."

"It wasn't Leon."

"I know; he's asleep. I wish—Well, anyway this is getaway money. I can get away from that son of a bitch now."

He'd suspected she felt that way; he was glad to be sure of it. Because it meant she wouldn't share the money—and the secret along with it—with Leon.

He said, "Then be sure you don't let him find that money, kid. And he might be awake when you go back. If you're smart you'll stash it somewhere first."

That was all he could do and now he wanted to get away as fast as he could, get back to his trailer and be in bed there before anybody found the body and raised an alarm. He finished his coffee as quickly as he could without burning himself and hurried back to the trailer.

He felt satisfied with what he'd done and glad he hadn't had a chance to kill Dolly. She was a good kid; she'd keep her mouth shut now.

Even without the bribe she wouldn't have been too likely, now that he thought of it, to go to the cops with her story. Carneys don't talk to cops about other carneys. But she would probably have talked to someone about it, Quintana or someone else, and the story, if it spread far enough, would have reached the cops eventually. But the money would keep her completely silent now.

He slept the moment his head touched the pillow.

CHAPTER THREE

Dr. Magus woke. Someone was shaking him, saying, "Doc, Doc," in a frantic whisper. A woman's voice; it sounded like that of Maybelle Seeley of the posing show.

"Go 'way," he said. "If I wake up you won't be there."

"Doc, this is Maybelle. I need you."

He was sure he was awake now. He rolled over on the bedroll and found he'd rolled against her knees; she was kneeling there beside him, a shadow in the dimness.

"You need me?" he said. "With hundreds of younger men on the lot, you need an old coot like me?"

The light tone, he knew, would calm her.

"Doc, somebody killed Mack Irby. I need your help."
He sat up. "Mack Irby? When? How?"

"It—it must have been about half an hour ago. They hit him over the head with something. The back of his head is—ugh."

He put an arm across her shoulders, pulled her down to a sitting position beside him. "Take it easy, gal. Where do you come in? Were you with him?"

"We were in Jesse's sleeping top. Mack rented it for all night. About half an hour ago we ran out of whisky and he pulled on his clothes and said he'd wake Pop and get us some. He crawled out under the flap and didn't come back. When it got to be a long time—my saying it was half an hour's just a guess—I got to remembering that I'd heard a kind of thunk sound just after he left and I got thinking he—well, maybe fell and hit his head. So I crawled out to look and there he was dead, just outside."

"Are you sure it wasn't a fall?"

"Yeah. It couldn't of been a fall, Doc."

"Had he been rolled? Wait, before you answer any more questions, you can use a drink if you haven't had one since you and he ran out. And I can too."

"Don't turn on a light, Doc. Somebody might find him any minute and—"

"I won't. I can find it in the dark." He groped his way to the foot locker, found the bottle and brought it back. He waited until they'd each taken a drink from it.

"All right now, was he rolled?"

"I—I don't—" Then defiantly. "Yes, he was. I wanted to know that too so I felt in his pockets. Just change. He usually carried his paper money in a roll but there wasn't any roll in his pants pockets. Or in his coat. He'd left his coat inside and I crawled back in and felt in it too. There was a folder that felt like it was traveler's checks, but it wasn't money."

"Ummm, he was rolled then, Maybelle. He'd have had more money on him in cash than just change. Who knows you were there with him?"

"Nobody, Doc, unless somebody saw me go in there and I don't think they did. And I didn't tell anybody. Unless he did, in advance before I went there and he was waiting for me."

"I doubt if he told anyone. Mack kept his business to himself, Maybelle. But he must have come around to the posing show to look you up and make the date. Didn't anyone see him talking to you there?"

"Huh-uh. He caught my eye from the outside of the tip, while we was ballying, and pointed around in back. After I got in, I ducked under the back canvas and we talked there."

"Good. Then they'll probably never get to you."

"Doc, they will, somehow. They'll know he had somebody there, he wouldn't of rented it just for himself, would he? And they'll find out it wasn't McGlassen or Trixie and—" Doc had his arm around her again and he felt her shiver. "Doc, I did tell both of them I had a heavy date tonight, after I saw Mack. They both hate me, one of them will cross me up with the cops if I try to say I was in my bunk, so I'll have to tell them I was with somebody, somebody who'll back up my story."

Dr. Magus smiled gently into the darkness. "A light begins to dawn. A lovely light." He cleared his throat.

"And far be it from me, my dear, to look a gift horse in the mouth, especially when the gift horse is so shapely a filly, but—"

"Yes, Doc?"

"Why is it so important to you to keep out of it? I mean, isn't the safest thing for you to do to go right now and wake up John Eckhart—he bunks right in the office car—and have him report the, ah, incident?"

"Doc, you couldn't of had much experience with cops if you think they'd let me off that easy. I been in trouble before, got a record—not much of a record but—"

"What for?"

"Just shoplifting. But three or four times and one time I had over a hundred bucks worth of stuff on me and that made it grand larceny instead of petty. I did six months for that. Doc, they'll throw the book at me. They won't figure I hit him over the head, no, but they'll figure I fingered him for whoever did kill him!"

"Right you are, Maybelle, I see it now. And on your own story, if you told them the truth, they could book you on a morals charge and use that to keep you on ice. But Maybelle, before I stick my neck out you don't mind if I doubt your word for a moment on one little thing?"

"I didn't kill him, Doc. And I don't know who did."

"Those two little points I do not doubt, my dear. I know you better than that. You are not a killer and you would not help one. But when it comes to money, money is something else again. Mack might or might not have been rolled before you, ah, looked to see. Or his money have been in his coat, or at least part of it might have been. And the killer had no access to his coat pockets, whereas you admit you looked through them. And since it would be more dangerous for me to give you an alibi if you have any Mack Irby money than if you haven't, will you overcome your maidenly modesty while I make one thousand per cent sure that you are not concealing so much as a sawbuck?"

She giggled a little. "Okay, Doc. It won't take you long to find out, me wearing only shoes and a wrapper."

"Good, and I remove the shoes first to save the best till last. No, nothing in the shoes. And now the wrapper . . . No, nothing. And now, keeping firmly in mind that money could be concealed, at least conceivably, upon any part of the body by being fastened down with adhesive tape, and that a tightly folded bill can be concealed, well, almost anywhere, and that it is too dark for me to see—" He missed no inch of surface, no nook or cranny. Maybelle giggled again. "Doc, no police matron ever gave me a search like that."

"No police matron would have the same ulterior motive. And you have no money on you but I found something just the same. I found how badly I want to give you an alibi for tonight. So if necessity arises wearing a blue uniform we shall say you slept here with me all night—and tell only half a lie. Oh, my dear—"

And Maybelle, all of whose amours had been with younger and less experienced men, learned a few things that night that she had never known before.

Young lust and then experienced lechery, with a murder in between. All in all, quite a night.

CHAPTER FOUR

Under blankets in the chill of early dawn, Dolly Quintana lay beside her husband, trembling not from cold but from fear. Fear of the very thought of what he would do to her if she ran away and he came after and found her. Not fear of death; she wouldn't be afraid to die, at least not to die a clean death, but killing wasn't what Leon had promised to do if she ever even tried to run away from him. It was acid. Acid thrown into her face to blind her and disfigure her so no other man would ever want her or touch her. She'd be blind and horrible looking and she wouldn't even be able to earn her living and she'd have to live out her life in eternal darkness in some institution, only she'd kill herself first—but that would be worse, harder to do, than if Leon killed her, and there'd be the pain and horror of the acid too. And he'd find her somewhere, sometime, no matter how far she ran or where she hid. He'd keep hunting till he found her. He was crazy jealous, really crazy.

She'd been so fiercely happy when Evans had given her that money, that two hundred and forty dollars, and now she lay there wishing that he hadn't. Because the money meant freedom but now she was finding out that she didn't have the courage to take it. The money was torture if all it did was show her her own cowardice.

But Leon wasn't bluffing about that acid. He had it, kept it in that horrible green bottle in his trunk. And if she took the bottle with her if she ran away that would only make her crazier. He'd get more, ten times as much, and come after her with it.

And if she didn't run away now the money was a danger. Oh God, if he found that money. He'd never believe anything she told him, the truth or a lie, about how she got it and even if he did he'd beat her anyway for holding out on him. There'd been the time when she'd found that purse with a five dollar bill in it and she'd thrown the purse away and kept the bill and had tucked it in her bra only Leon had found it because something—probably he'd been watching the bally for the model show or maybe looking at some of those books with dirty pictures he'd told her Evans had— had made him want her in the daytime and he'd almost torn the clothes off her instead of letting her undress herself so he'd found the money, and he'd beaten her up instead of laying her and he'd accused her of whoring and he might have killed her if she hadn't managed to get him to listen long enough to tell him about the purse and he'd gone to see if it was where she said she'd thrown it and thank God it was still there, a woman's little red purse just like she'd described it so he believed her finally about that but still wouldn't believe she hadn't told him about it because she'd wanted to buy him a present for a surprise, and he said she'd had the beating coming anyway for holding out on him, and that had been over only five dollars and this was two hundred and forty. He might even kill her for that instead of just beating her, but anyway there'd been one good thing about that beating the day he'd found the five dollars he'd never got around to doing what he'd started to do to her, there was a call to bally first, and he'd have probably hurt her worse doing that to her when he felt that way than he'd hurt her beating her, he hadn't been so bad that way at first but now he never enjoyed having her unless he was hurting her. Oh, she'd loved him at first and had even enjoyed being hurt a little, just a little, when he had her but it kept getting worse all the time like his jealousy and now there wasn't any love left for him, just fear, and she hated it every time he touched her only she had to pretend or else, oh God wouldn't it be wonderful just once to have a man make love to her and treat her gently, why almost anybody on the lot even that Evans, he'd killed somebody tonight but he'd be gentler with her than Leon, anybody on the lot if only she dared, but especially Joe

Linder, she could really love Joe Linder, and he wanted her too, she could tell, she could feel it just the way he looked at her any time Leon wasn't watching his face, she could feel his wanting her and it was a good kind of wanting, if only she could live with him instead of Leon, or even one night but don't even think about it because it couldn't be, forget it. God, it would be awful if Leon found that money but he wouldn't because she'd taken Evans' advice and stashed it before she'd come back here, not in too good a place and somebody might find it there before she could get it but at least nobody would know it was she who hid it there, and tomorrow, today rather, when Leon went into town like he'd said he was going to buy a new silk shirt—he always wore bright colored silk shirts for his act—she could get the money back from its temporary hiding place if it was still there and with time to do it she could hide it in a place where he'd never find it in a million years, and right in his own trunk not hers because she knew he sometimes looked through her trunk when she wasn't there, but he had that old cornet of his at the bottom of his trunk, the one he used to play a long time ago, he hadn't touched it for years and it was broken too but he kept it at the bottom of his trunk because he was superstitious about it for some reason and the roll of bills would slip right down in the horn and—

There was a babble of voices from outside the canvas, quite a distance away. It sounded like a lot of people all talking at once and excitedly. Leon must have been partly awake because he heard it too and sat up.

"What the hell's that?" he asked.

And Suddenly Dolly had an idea what it might be because those voices could come from behind the penny arcade top and it had been near there that she'd seen Evans with the tent stake before he'd turned around and thrown it back into the darkness. So now she'd know soon whom he'd killed back there last night. She hoped it wasn't someone she knew and liked. It occurred to her now—she hadn't even wondered before—that it could even have been Joe Linder. God, dear God, don't let it be Joe Linder.

She said, "I don't know, Leon. Want me to go see?" She didn't want to go see but she offered to because then he'd probably say no; if she didn't offer he'd probably tell her to go.

"You stay here," he growled. "I'll see what's going on."

He pulled on trousers and a shirt and went under the canvas sidewall. He was gone ten or fifteen minutes. When he came back he started to undress to get back under the blankets and didn't say anything till she asked him what had happened.

"Mack Irby," he said. "The guy that was talker for the unborn show until he was in that accident a couple months ago. Somebody killed him and rolled him."

"I remember him. But I didn't know he was back."

"I didn't either. They say he just got back, late last night. Now shut up. I want to get another couple hours sleep. It's only five o'clock."

He lay down and then sat up again suddenly, staring at her. "Say, you here in bed all last night?"

"Sure, Leon. Why?"

"Because he'd had some dame with him in Jesse Rau's sleeping top, that's why. Nobody knows who it was. I was just wondering."

"Well, you can stop wondering. It sure as hell wasn't me. I didn't even know the guy except by sight and I didn't even know he was back."

"All right, all right."

He lay down again, apparently satisfied. But she shivered, knowing that now—unless it came out who really had been with Mack Irby—he'd brood about it all day and suspect more and more that it had been she.

Why, she wondered suddenly, had Evans killed Mack Irby? For money? Was the money he had given her money he'd taken off the man he killed? But that would hardly be it; Evans made too good money to kill a man to pick his pockets. Lived in a trailer of his own and had a good income. No, it must have been over a woman. Leon had said that Irby'd had a woman with him in Rau's sleeping top. Well, it wasn't any business of hers. Evans must have had some good reason, and even if he hadn't given her that money, she'd probably not tell anybody.

She had enough worries of her own, and Mack Irby had been nothing to her. She knew who he was; that's all.

No, it was none of her business. Whether Leon would start to suspect and brood again now, that was enough for her to worry about. She was afraid that he would. Was there any possibility that he'd find out? A few beads of sweat came out on her forehead as she realized suddenly that there was definitely a chance of it. There'd be a police investigation of that murder and the police would be asking questions of everybody on the lot, checking who had been out and around at about the time of the murder. And they could tell from examining the body what time he'd been killed, she knew that from reading detective stories, and he must have been killed just before she'd seen Evans so they'd be particularly interested in who was awake and around at that time, and they'd ask Hank at the chow top who'd been in there eating between, say, two and three o'clock, and if Hank remembered she'd been there—and he probably would because she'd sat at a table instead of the counter and he'd had to walk over to take her order and then to bring it and collect for it—they'd come to ask her whom she'd seen on the midway. And they might question her right in front of Leon. Or they might question Leon separately to see if he could tell them what time she'd left and come back and he'd learn that she'd been out on the midway when she'd just told him she'd stayed in bed all night.

She prayed a little, Please God, don't let Leon find out I was out last night.

Even without that, she realized now, she was in for a terrible day and evening. Now that Leon had once asked if she'd been the woman with Mack Irby, he'd go on brooding about it more and more all day and when she stood in front of the board this afternoon and evening for him to throw the knives at her he'd do like he always did when he'd been brooding, throw them closer than usual, dangerously closer, to punish and frighten her.

If only it would rain today, if only it would rain so they wouldn't open. She prayed a little again, this time: Oh, Lord, please make it rain today, please make it rain.

The sun came out bright and the day was pleasant.

CHAPTER FIVE

Cops. the lot was full of cops. There seemed to be dozens of them although actually there were only four.

They got to Dr. Magus a little after ten o'clock. Rather, one of them did. A lieutenant in plain clothes that might just as well have been a uniform from the look of him. Mother-naked you'd still have spotted him for a cop.

But not a tough one. Despite his size, six feet one and two hundred thirty pounds, he was soft-spoken, gentle. For a cop, smart. Showalter, his name was, Lieutenant Showalter. Dr. Magus found that he liked him. Not strange really because Dr. Magus liked just about everybody, even cops if they didn't throw their weight around.

The lieutenant sat now with an open notebook on the little table in the mitt camp and Dr. Magus, not wanting to sit across from him as though telling his fortune, sat on the foot locker off to one side. The lieutenant poised his pencil.

"Your name?"

"Dr. Magus."

"I mean your real name."

Dr. Magus smiled. "I've almost forgotten it, Lieutenant. And I'd much prefer to forget. But since you'll no doubt suspect me of being an escaped convict, I suppose I shall have to tell you. The name is Morris, Raymond L. Morris. If I recall aright, the L stands for Leroy. And I was born under the sign of Scorpio in the year 1900 and in the town of Green Bay, Wisconsin."

"Got a record, Morris?"

"Please call me Doc. The title is almost genuine."

"What do you mean, 'almost genuine'?"

"It would have been Doctor of Philosophy, not of Medicine, but at the age of twenty-three I was within four months of acquiring that degree when a youthful peccadillo caused my expulsion from the august halls of learning. I have, of course, a master's degree, psychology major, but I presume you would not want to call me Master."

The lieutenant said, "I'll settle for Doc. And the record?"

"Nothing really worth mentioning. A few fines for fortune telling in places where the law frowns upon my profession. A few other and minor misdemeanors."

"Done time?"

"Fifty-two years of it, but none behind bars. In front of bars, quite a bit."

"How well did you know Mack Irby?"

"Merely a casual acquaintance. And as to when I saw him last, which is what you'd ask me next if I do not anticipate the question, it would have been late yesterday evening, somewhere in the neighborhood of eleven o'clock. He'd just returned; from what I hear, he couldn't have been on the lot more than fifteen or twenty minutes. Is that right?"

"Yeah. His train got in at ten twenty-five. He took a taxi to the lot, so he'd have got here about a quarter to eleven. Where did you see him?"

"Here. He dropped in merely to pass the time of evening. I gave him a drink, but he stayed only a minute."

"You didn't see him after that?"

"Not even the empty shell from which his soul had fled. I fear that I slept through the commotion which I hear accompanied the finding of his body early this morning. It had been taken away by the time I was up and about. Who found him, by the way?"

"A halfwit named Sammy. Doesn't have any last name, or so he says. What do you know about Sammy?"

"Almost nothing except that I like him. He's done errands for me a few times. He works for Jesse Rau, who runs the milk bottle game. Sammy sets up the bottles when they're knocked down. He seems to have the requisite mentality to perform that task."

"After Irby left did you stay in this tent all night?"

"I did."

"You didn't go outside once, not even to go to the doniker?"

"I see you are picking up carney slang already, Lieutenant. No, I did not go to the doniker. But if you want to make a very fine point of whether I remained within these canvas walls, I recall that once I stepped under the back one and a few feet beyond it. On business, let us say, but not sufficiently serious business to require a longer walk than that since it was in the middle of the night."

"About what time?"

"I haven't the faintest idea. Why would it matter?"

"It might if you saw anybody while you were out there. Did you?"

"Not a soul."

"You spent the night alone?"

"On the contrary, Lieutenant. I enjoyed—and I use the word advisedly—very pleasant company."

"Who?"

"I fear it would be indiscreet for me to answer that. Unless of course the young lady in question has already told you she spent the night with me, in which case I shall be glad to confirm her story."

"She has. And otherwise, Doc, there's suspicion she may have been the dame who was with Irby last night."

"Very well. Then I spent the night with the young lady who told you she spent the night with me."

"That won't do, Doc. Maybe she didn't but if I told you the name first you'd say she did just to give her an alibi. It wouldn't mean anything if I told you first."

"You have a point there, Lieutenant. My companion last night was Maybelle Seeley. And again to anticipate a question, she came here, by prearrangement, somewhere around midnight and she left somewhere around eight o'clock this morning."

"She was here all the time?"

"Yes, she was. I will not strain your credulity by claiming that I, at my age, was awake all night. But I am a very light sleeper; she could not possibly have left and returned without my knowing it."

"A light sleeper? The commotion over finding Irby's body didn't wake you this morning."

"Lieutenant, that was on the other side of the midway, around behind the penny arcade top. I would hazard the guess that the distance between here and there is two hundred yards. I doubt if I could have heard voices at that distance even if I had been wide awake and listening for them. By the way, Lieutenant, you said that there is—or, I hope, was—suspicion that Miss Seeley was with Irby last night. May I ask why?"

"Some dame was with him and we haven't found out who yet. And he talked to her around in back of the model show tent."

"Yes, she mentioned to me that he had talked to her briefly. And why not? Maybelle had been, ah, going steady with Charlie Flack, who was killed in the same accident in which Irby was injured. He wanted to tell her how sorry he was that Charlie had been killed."

"So she told us. Okay, but since it wasn't Maybelle, have you got any idea who it could have been he took to that tent?"

"Please, Lieutenant, do not continue to use the word tent; it hurts my ears. There are no tents on a carnival lot; they are all tops, from a sleeping top on up, there is not a tent among them. No, I have no idea who, if anyone, he took to the sleeping top."

"He had somebody there. Otherwise why'd he rent it from Rau? Irby had a bedroll of his own, still over at the Mystery of Sex show he used to be barker for."

"Talker for, Lieutenant. More specifically grinder for, since a show that operates continuously and without a bally doesn't require a spiel. But yes, I agree that if Mack Irby had intended to sleep alone he could have done so almost anywhere and without renting the bridal suite. But it is possible that he rented it in advance, in hope, and he might have been disappointed in that hope."

The lieutenant grunted agreement, as Dr. Magus hoped he would. He had coached Maybelle very carefully in her story, had told her to volunteer—lest someone had seen or heard them talking—the information that she had talked to Irby, and the further information that he had made a pass at her and had told her he'd rented Rau's top and wanted her to spend the night with him there. But that she'd turned him down because of a previous commitment if for no other reason.

He pushed home the advantage. "From what I hear, Lieutenant, Irby was in funds and a few dollars would not have mattered to him, so it is not unlikely that he would have rented that top merely in the hope that he could have company therein. He may even have had Maybelle in mind, among others. But if he made such a suggestion to her she didn't tell me about it. However it is not unprobable that whether he had one particular woman in mind or was willing to settle for one of several—as seems likely after seven weeks' continence in the hospital—he might have been unable at so late an hour, on such short notice, to find a woman who was both free and willing to help him break his fast."

The lieutenant grunted again.

Dr. Magus asked, "But if he did have a woman there why is her identity important? You don't think a woman killed him, do you?"

"Not likely, with a tent stake. It isn't a woman's weapon. We found the tent stake, still with traces of blood and hair on it. The murderer had carried it with him until he got almost to the midway alongside the penny arcade tent-top. And besides, Irby was struck down just outside the sleeping top and he hadn't been dragged. From the position we figure he crawled out and was struck down just as he started to get to his feet. But about the woman, if there was one she could have fingered him for the job, couldn't she? She could know or think he was loaded with dough, see? And she could arrange before she went there with him—or went to meet him there, whichever it was—to have a man waiting outside to slug him when he came out. And if he didn't go out for any reason of his own, she could have pretended to be thirsty and talked him into going out so he'd get it."

Dr. Magus nodded. "Could have been that way, if there was a woman with him. Know what time he was killed?"

"Coroner says somewhere around two o'clock, give or take an hour. Examined him at six o'clock and said he'd been dead somewhere around four hours."

"You said something, Lieutenant, about his being loaded with dough. Have you been able to find out?"

"We know how much he must have had within a few dollars. We phoned Glenrock and the boys there checked it right away. With the hospital and other places. Had a hundred and twenty-seven bucks on him when he was admitted to the hospital. Their guess is he averaged spending about ten bucks a week for the seven weeks he was there—cigarettes and other stuff he could send out for—so he left there two o'clock yesterday afternoon with somewhere around fifty-five bucks cash and an insurance company check for two thousand. Went right to the Glenrock bank and cashed it but took eighteen hundred in traveler's checks. Gives him two hundred fifty-five, give or take a little according to how good their guess is at the hospital on how much he spent for incidentals while he was there. Caught a 4:10 train out of Glenrock, came right here. Figure his ticket, meal on the train, taxi fare, bottle or two of whisky, say twenty bucks. He'd have had about two hundred thirty-five. And the traveler's checks, but they were still in his pocket."

Dr. Magus said, "How disappointed someone must have been, if the someone knew about that insurance settlement and thought he might be carrying two thousand cash on him."

"Did you think that?"

"I'd heard—and I've forgotten where but it was the general rumor around the lot—that Mack got a settlement from an insurance company on the accident. But I certainly wouldn't have figured him as stupid and careless enough to carry it on him in cash. Does your question indicate that I am a suspect?"

The lieutenant grinned. "Doc, you're the only guy around here I've talked to that hasn't acted like I got leprosy or something. Maybe that ought to make me suspicious of you, that and the fact that you've pumped me into doing more talking than you have. But you just don't look to me like a guy who'd use a tent stake."

"Thank you kindly."

"Not at all. If this was a con game setup instead of a bashing you'd be my first choice. What's an unborn show?"

Dr. Magus smiled. "An unborn show is a collection of fetuses in glass jars. It is also known as a punk show and the fetuses are known as pickled punks. Whatever the grind is, that's the joint. Usually they are human fetuses in various stages of development, but occasionally there will be an animal fetus if it's a freak one. I believe Burt's unborn show, the Mystery of Sex, has the fetus of a two-headed calf. But that's just an extra attraction, the pitch is on the Iranian fetuses - male and female, naked and unadorned. Which, of course, they are."

"Fake or real?"

"Probably quite real because they'd be cheaper to get. It's carney tradition to kid an unborn show man about the Goodyear trade marks on the kiesters of his pickled punks, but it's just a stock gag. Think what they'd cost, whereas the human fetus has no market value—except possibly in parts of Mexico where I am told they are used in making tamales, although that is possibly apocryphal. But anyone who has a friend in the right spot in a hospital or morgue can get all the fetuses he wants for a few drinks or at most a few bucks apiece."

"That's all there is in the Mystery of Sex show?"

"Practically all. There is also a pair of flashy wall charts of male and female anatomy in cross section, no doubt to show, in the case of the female, where a fetus comes from and, in the case of the male, how it gets there. And there is also and more important, a table with a stack of sex books on it. That's where the profits come from. It's why the unborn show has the low admission of one thin dime, that's to get the marks on the inside where they become a captive audience for Burt's pitch. The books sell for two bucks apiece. But they tell everything, Burt says."

The lieutenant closed his notebook—in which the only thing he'd written was Dr. Magus's real name— and stood up.

"That's my next stop," he said, "so thanks for the briefing."

"Have you met Burt?"

The lieutenant shook his head. "Nope."

Dr. Magus grinned. "If you tell him I sent you, he might tell you what time it is, if you ask him nicely. Otherwise—say, he's probably still in the chow top. I got back from there just before you came and Burt had just come in."

"Okay, I'll look there. How'll I know him?"

"The guy who gives you the dirtiest look."

"Seriously."

"All right. Let's see. Medium size, about forty, getting bald on top but he's got his hat on so that won't help you. Dresses fairly well. Oh, I remember. He's wearing a brown suit, tan silk shirt, solid color maroon tie."

"Good," the lieutenant said. "But listen, Doc, will you try to remember who it was told you Irby got a settlement from an insurance company?"

"I'll try, but why are you interested?"

"Because I can't find, or haven't found yet, that anybody here communicated with him while he was in the hospital, but somebody must have or how'd it get known around the lot? Some of 'em even knew the amount."

"But, Lieutenant, it would matter only negatively, wouldn't it?"

"I don't get you, Doc."

"I mean that if whoever did have the word direct intended to kill Irby for his two thousand dollars, the last thing he'd have done would have been to spread the news that Irby was coming back loaded. He'd have kept that news to himself so nobody would beat him to it."

The lieutenant rubbed the back of his neck. "Maybe you got something there. Well, be seeing you."

After the lieutenant had gone, Dr. Magus went over to the little table and sat down by it. He felt thoughtful but he didn't know what he was thoughtful about.

Certainly not about what had puzzled Lieutenant Showalter; he could have told Showalter exactly how the insurance money story had started and exactly how and it had become more specific.

A week or more ago Mack Irby had sent Burt a postcard. It had told Burt that he'd be back before the end of the season to pick up his possessions but that he didn't expect his job back, and added that he was getting a good settlement from the insurance company.

Burt had showed or mentioned the card to several people. But why should Dr. Magus have told the lieutenant? If Burt wanted to tell him, he would.

And the same went for Barney King. He'd had coffee with Barney an hour ago and Barney had told him how Mack Irby had stopped at the ticket booth last night and had talked a while, mentioning two grand as the amount of the settlement he'd received. And Barney, an hour later, had mentioned it in the poker game in the G-top.

So the lieutenant's curiosity would be satisfied if Burt and Barney chose to tell him those facts, and the lieutenant was heading for the unborn show now. If they didn't choose to tell him that was their business.

But that wasn't what Dr. Magus was feeling thoughtful about. Nor was it, quite, wondering who really had killed Mack Irby. Except as a matter of curiosity, and idle curiosity at that, he didn't care a rideboy's damn who had killed Irby. But something was stirring at the back of his mind and he wanted to know what it was.

He pulled over the madball, the two-inch diameter crystal in its silver stand, and polished it lovingly with a square of black velvet. He smiled a little, thinking how descriptive was the carney slang word for it, madball.

He stared at it, but not into it, musingly.

Round like the world, he thought. Like the world, sometimes seeming transparent, easy to see through; like the world, at other times mysterious and a little frightening. Not that he ever really saw anything there except once in a while when he was a little drunk and then it always scared him, but looking into it helped him to concentrate.

Usually, that is. This time it didn't. Whatever the thought that he'd been on the verge of thinking, it slipped farther and farther away.

CHAPTER SIX

Mid-evening and Sammy was glad because Jesse was drinking and when Jesse started drinking on the job he nearly always closed the place early, even if business was fairly good like tonight, and if he closed Sammy wouldn't have to set up any more milk bottles and might even have the rest of the evening to do anything he wanted to do. Sometimes when he was drinking Jesse would go off by himself and he'd tell Sammy to stick on the lot and not get in any trouble but as long as he stayed on the lot Sammy would be free to wander around and see the other games and the shows.

Tonight Sammy was especially glad that they might close early because Jesse was mad at him. Jesse had bawled the holy hell out of him this morning and had been acting mean to him ever since, all because he'd found a man dead and instead of pretending he hadn't found a man dead he'd called people to tell them about it. And it wasn't fair of Jesse to be mad because how could Sammy have known, since he'd never found a dead man before, that he was supposed to go away quickly and let somebody else find the man?

That was the bad thing, you never knew what you were supposed to do when something new happened until it had happened once and you'd learned, but the first time you probably did the wrong thing and so many new things kept happening that you were always in trouble because you'd done wrong on them.

And Jesse was always getting mad and bawling him out for something even though he always tried to do his best for Jesse because Jesse took care of him and Jesse always told him that if he ever quit taking care of him they'd come and put him in a place behind bars because he couldn't take care of himself. And Sammy knew Jesse was telling the truth because he'd been in a place like that once, a place with bars on the windows and the doors always locked. He'd hated it there. And one day there'd been a door open and he'd walked out and there had been a horrible time, he didn't know how many days, with people kicking him around and ordering him away and slamming doors on him when he was hungry, starving to death and hardly able to walk. And then he'd heard music and there was the carnival lot and he'd walked the midway dazzled by the bright colors and the happy music and tortured by the smell of frying hamburgers. And then Jesse had yelled "Hey, kid!" at him and from that moment everything had been all right. Jesse had asked him if he wanted to set up milk bottles and earn a little money and it had been hard for him to learn just how to do it right—well, it hadn't been hard to learn how to set them up but it had been awfully hard to learn when to set them up, to wait until the man had thrown three baseballs instead of putting back one milk bottle if he knocked it over on the first or second throw. He had to learn to watch and count the baseballs, one, two, three, and after that he could put back any of the milk bottles that had been knocked down. But Jesse had growled and sworn at him until he'd learned. And then after a while Jesse had taken him over to the place where the carney's ate and had bought him a meal and he'd eaten it so fast that Jesse had stared at him and said, "Damn it, kid, when did you eat last?" and when he said he didn't remember Jesse had bought him a second meal and his stomach was finally filled. That night Jesse had taken him to the little green tent that he'd learned was a sleeping top and had said they'd sleep together, and something had happened that night that had hurt him, hurt him bad, but Jesse had fed him and so anything Jesse wanted to do to him was all right, anything. That had been about a year ago, he thought, anyway there had been one winter since it happened, and he'd been with Jesse ever since.

And Jesse bought him all he wanted to eat, always, and if Jesse never gave him any money, that didn't matter much because there wasn't anything he ever needed money for except cotton candy and he could get money for that sometimes by doing errands for other carneys sometimes when Jesse didn't need him. Right now he had fifty cents in his pocket, burning a hole there, that Mr. Linder had given him early this afternoon for going to a store a block from the lot and bringing back some things Mr. Linder had written down on a list for the Store Man to read. But when Sammy got back Jesse had made him start work right away so he hadn't had time to spend the fifty cents. That was another reason he hoped Jesse would close early tonight because then the Cotton Candy Lady would still be in her booth and he could have five big balls of fluffy cotton candy without having to wait until tomorrow for them. The Cotton Candy Lady charged the marks fifteen cents for a cone of cotton candy but she always gave them to Sammy for a dime if Sammy waited till a time when there weren't any other customers there.

And now Jesse took the bottle out from under the counter and drank again and this time he drank the last of the little that was left in it and threw down the empty bottle. And sure enough he said, "Okay, kid, let's knock it off. We done enough today." And it was still early enough that everything else in the carney was running, maybe only about ten o'clock or even earlier. And now if only Jesse didn't want to go to the sleeping top he could have those cotton candies.

Sammy started to lower the canvas front of the booth and he remembered something he'd been wondering.

"Jesse," he said. He'd called Jesse Mr. Jesse at first, like he called everybody else Mr. or Miss but Jesse hadn't liked it and had made him stop.

"Yeah?"

"Jesse, how old am I?"

"Hell, I don't know. Eighteen, maybe twenty. Why?"

"The cop asked me. When he was asking about me finding the man dead. I didn't know but I been wondering. How many is eighteen?"

"Goddam, what you get not minding your own business. You do anything like that again—"

Sammy cringed for fear Jesse was going to get mad all over again and even hit him. He said, "I won't, Jesse."

"Goddam well better not. Aw right, run along and do whatever you wanta, long as you stick on the lot. I'm gonna take the boys with the dice tonight."

Jesse went out under the sidewall.

Sammy straightened things up, put all the baseballs into the foot locker and locked it, picked up the bottle Jesse had thrown down and pushed it out under the back canvas, then pulled out the plug that turned off the lights.

And Sammy was free.

A few minutes later he was eating his first cone of cotton candy and while he ate it he watched the bally of the model show across the way. They were starting to bally again when he got his second cone and with it in his hand he wandered over closer to watch.

Miss Trixie and Miss Maybelle were on the platform in their silk wrappers. They were both pretty but Sammy watched Miss Trixie. He liked Miss Trixie; she gave him quarters for doing errands for her two or three times a week. And she treated him nice. Some of the other women on the lot acted as though they didn't like to have him around but Miss Trixie didn't seem to mind. She was small and had such smooth nice black hair and such red lips.

Her silk wrapper was pulled tight around her and in front there were two mounds that were breasts. Other women had them too and he wondered why. For the first time Sammy found himself wondering why women were different from men. Of course, Sammy and Jesse had breasts too, after a fashion, but not the kind women had. What were they good for? Most men, he knew, liked to see women's breasts and the rest of women's bodies, too; that was why the marks paid money to go in the model show, to see the models take off their robes and pose on a little stage, in only a G-string and a thin cheeseclothy bra that you could see right through, and he knew that in some towns they got by without wearing even the net bras but they always had to wear the G-strings when they posed. But why did men pay money to see women pose that way? He'd asked Jesse once when Jesse had been in a good mood and Jesse couldn't tell him; Jesse had said, "Damn if I know either, kid," and had sounded as though he meant it, although you couldn't always tell with Jesse.

Sammy had never gone inside the model show, not even inside the top when a show wasn't going on, because Jesse had told him not to. But once he'd seen Miss Trixie in just the costume she posed in, the G-string and the net bra. It had been on a hot night, an awfully hot night, a couple of months ago in the middle of summer. It had been one of the nights Jesse had closed early and Sammy had been free and he'd been walking around behind the tops and Miss Trixie, in a robe, had ducked under the sidewall of the model show top and had called to him. She'd given him fifty cents and told him to go to the grab joint, not all the way to the chow top but just to the grab joint, and get her a coney island sandwich with everything on and to get himself one too if he was hungry or else keep the quarter. He'd been a little hungry so he got two coney island sandwiches with everything on and called to Miss Trixie from in back like she'd told him to, and she'd come back under the sidewall again and stood with him while they ate the sandwiches. And after a minute she'd said, "Is that a breeze?" and had taken off her robe and hung it over a tent rope and stood there almost naked enjoying the slight breeze that had just come up, and he'd seen her body. It was whiter and smoother than a man's and somehow different in some way. And in two other ways the difference wasn't hard to tell at all. One of those ways was her breasts. Of course he'd known women had mounds there on their chests because you could tell that much even when they were wearing dresses or robes, but seeing Miss Trixie's breasts that close and with only a thin net that you could see right through over them, Sammy realized for the first time that they were breasts like his own except that the nipples were bigger and the breasts themselves were a lot bigger. Like swellings. But they were pretty and he liked them and looking at them gave him a funny feeling, as though he wanted to do something but didn't know what it was he wanted to do.

The other difference between her body and a man's was even more puzzling and it was the other way around; Miss Trixie's G-string was so small and fitted against her so tightly that he could see she was different there too, that she didn't have what men had there, and he wondered if all women were like Miss Trixie there and if so what they did when they went to the doniker, and he'd wanted to ask Miss Trixie about it.

He'd forgotten all about it until now, staring up at Miss Trixie on the platform, he remembered and started wondering again about the mystery of women.

He wondered how he could find out about such things, who he could ask who might tell him. And suddenly it came to him where he could find out and without even having to ask anybody and it was so simple that Sammy wondered why he'd never thought of it before.

Because he remembered now the word sex. He'd heard people use it and he didn't know exactly what it meant but he did know that it had something to do with women and their bodies. And the unborn show was named Mystery of Sex, wasn't it? And didn't Mr. King, the talker for the show, say that the mystery of sex was explained inside, everything about it, the naked truth. And Sammy knew what naked meant, it meant without any clothes on at all, not even a bra or a G-string. Why, if he went in that show he could learn everything, and why couldn't he go in tonight, why couldn't he? He still had three dimes left out of his fifty cents and the unborn show—what did unborn mean? Well, he'd find that out too—cost only one dime so he could have two more cotton candies and still go to the show.

His second cotton candy was finished now, though, so he went back to the booth and waited until the Cotton Candy Lady wasn't busy and then bought his third one from her. She smiled at him and made it a bigger one than usual. She said, "Sammy, if everybody loved cotton candy like you do, I'd be rich." And she pushed back his dime. "This one's on the house, Sammy, if you go get me a san'wich. I'm starvin'."

She gave him a quarter. "Hamburger. Tell him don't skimp the mustard."

When Sammy came back with it for her his cotton candy was gone again and he wanted to buy another. But she laughed and gave him that one for free too. So he still had three dimes.

He'd been wanting to use one of them for something and for a while he couldn't remember what and just wandered down the midway. Then he heard Mr. King talking in front of the unborn show and he remembered.

" . . . see everything, boys, I mean everything, the sex mystery exposed, red hot, sex in the raw, everything explained, plain down to earth unadorned, right before your very eyes, now it can be told, what papa did to mama, one dime only one dime, come and see for yourselves, the mystery of sex, only a dime, continuous . . ." Sammy dropped the paper cone that had held his fourth cotton candy, stepped up to the ticket box and put a dime on the counter. Mr. King reached for the dime, then looked at Sammy. He pushed the dime back.

He said, "Hell, kid, you're with it. You don't got to pay. Just walk on in."

Sammy said, "Thanks, Mr. King," and started around the ticket box. But then Mr. King said, "Wait a minute," and he stopped.

Mr. King said, "Listen, Sammy—your name's Sammy, ain't it?"

Sammy nodded.

"Well, Sammy, I just thought. You don't want to go in there now. Burt's got some marks in there and you might queer his pitch on the books, see?"

Sammy didn't see, but he knew it meant he couldn't go in now. He said, "But sometime can I go in, Mr. King?"

"Sure, Sammy. Tell you when. Come around early afternoon some time just when we're opening and there ain't any biz yet. Then go in and stay as long as you want. Or hell, come before we're open if you just want to look around. Just so you don't touch nothing. But kid, there's nothing in there you'd want to see. Just pickled punks."

"What are pickled punks, Mr. King?"

"Fetuses. Babies that never got born. Dead and pickled in jars and what you want to see them for anyway?"

"I don't want to look at no babies, Mr. King. But I want to see what you said, I mean about what sex is and naked and things like that."

Mr. King shook his head slowly and sadly. "Believe you me, Sammy, if you're starting that far behind scratch you won't learn a damn thing in there; it'd just confuse the hell out of you. Listen, you really mean you don't know anything about sex?"

"No, Mr. King."

"I'll be damned. But take my word for it, Sammy, this isn't where to find out. And for that matter I ain't the guy to tell you, because you ought to be showed and not told. Get a dame to show you sometime."

"Show me what, Mr. King?"

"The most wonderful thing on earth, Sammy. And you sure look old enough to be showed."

"Would any woman show me? Do you think Miss Trixie would?"

Mr. King chuckled. "I don't know about any woman, kid, you'd better be careful who you ask. But I guess Trixie would, for enough money. But that's the catch, kid, that dame's money hungry. You can get it better and—" He looked at Sammy again. "Well, maybe not for free but cheaper'n Trixie'd take you for."

Then a group of people started by and Mr. King didn't look at Sammy any more; he was looking at the people and talking into the microphone. "This way, boys, this way to the sex show, and only a dime to see . . . "

And Sammy wandered off. Still with three thin dimes he went back and spent one of them for his fifth cotton candy, and the model show was ballying again and Miss Trixie was on the platform and he watched her some more. Wondering what the most wonderful thing on earth was and how much money he'd have to have for her to show it to him.

Certainly, from the way Mr. King had spoken, it would be more than the two dimes he had left. Probably it meant paper money, folding money, and Sammy had never had a piece of paper money in his life, ever. Not of his own, anyway; sometimes when he was sent on an errand he was given paper money to buy something and brought back change from it. Maybe if he saved all the money, the hard money, people gave him once in a while for doing errands until he got a lot of it, a whole handful of it, somebody would give him paper money for it. But that didn't seem likely. People gave you hard money in change out of folding money but why should they give you paper money for hard money?

No, it just didn't seem likely that he'd ever have folding money, not unless he stole it. And Jesse had told him not to steal. Jesse had said, "There ain't nuttin' wrong with stealing, kid, if you can get away with it. But you're too Goddam dumb to know what yuh can get away with and what yuh can't. So lay off or yuh'll get in trouble. Get me?" And Sammy always tried to do what Jesse told him because Jesse fed him and took care of him so he could never get paper money by stealing it.

He finished his cotton candy and, although he still had two more dimes left, he didn't seem to want any more of it just then. And Trixie had gone inside the model show top because they weren't ballying any more. The show must be going on inside now and he wished he could go inside and see it because he wondered just how they posed in there and what they did, but he remembered Jesse had told him never to go in there. And anyway maybe his two dimes wouldn't be enough.

He wandered the midway again and because he might as well do something with his two dimes he rode twice on the merry-go-round, which next to cotton candy was his favorite way of spending money people gave him for doing errands, although he rode the merry-go-round only if he'd had all the cotton candy he wanted or if the Cotton Candy Lady wasn't in her booth.

After that he didn't have any more money to worry about and he just wandered. On the midway for a while and then around behind the tops. Back where the trailers and the trucks and the living tops were. He wanted to find someone to talk to but everybody must have been busy on the midway because he couldn't find anybody.

There was a light on, though, in one of the trailers. Mr. Evans's trailer. He knocked on the door and when there wasn't any answer he tried the knob and it wasn't locked, so he went in. Mr. Evans wouldn't care and Mr. Evans always had magazines with pictures in them and he'd already let Sammy look at pictures in those magazines so he wouldn't care if Sammy looked at them again.

But there weren't any magazines lying out in sight so they must be in one of the cabinets built into the wall of the trailer. He opened a cabinet door at random and it was the right cabinet the first time. The magazines were there.

He took them over to the table and sat looking at them for a while, at the pictures of strange places and people doing strange things. Some of the pictures were interesting but most of them weren't. When he had looked at pictures long enough and found himself getting restless he wanted to put the magazines away but now he couldn't remember exactly which cabinet he'd opened and found them in. He should have left it open, but he'd closed it again. It could have been any one of several.

But he'd know it because it would be empty; there'd been nothing in it except the magazines and he'd taken the whole stack of them out.

The first cabinet he tried wasn't the right one. It had clothes and linens in it. The second he tried was a smaller one; he should have realized it was too small and the wrong shape to hold the stack of magazines lying flat but he'd opened it before that occurred to him. And he saw that there were books in it, about a dozen books of different shapes and sizes, some of them looking expensive and fancy, others paper bound and dog-eared. Sammy wondered if there were pictures in the books. He couldn't remember ever having happened to look for pictures in a book and there might be. He pulled out the biggest and most expensive looking of the books.

The pictures in the book were different from pictures in magazines. The first one he turned to was a picture of a man and a woman both naked and in a strange position. Strange, anyway, to Sammy. And he turned pages and saw more pictures, lots of pictures, and they were all different and some of them pretty complicated but most of them were pictures of a man and woman naked together. Sammy took the book over to the table and began to study the pictures carefully, because he knew that this was the answer to what he'd been wondering about.

He studied the pictures and found within himself a growing excitement, a kind of excitement he hadn't known existed. It made him feel funny, looking at those pictures. Some of the pictures were puzzling because it seemed there was more than one thing a man and a woman could do together but in most of the pictures they were doing the same thing in slightly different ways and that one thing at least was clear to him.

This was it, this was the show he'd come to see, here's where he saw it, male and female naked and unadorned, the mystery of sex, right before his eyes, the naked truth, and not even for one thin dime but for free, doctors and nurses and Sammy admitted free, continuous performance and stay as long as you like, educational, plain down to earth unadorned, what papa did to mama, educational, now going on, here's where you see it all.

Sammy stayed long enough to look at all the pictures in all the books—although some of the books didn't have any pictures, just printing, so he didn't waste time on them, and pictures in some of the books that did have pictures were just pictures of naked women instead of men and women both in the same picture, and those weren't as interesting.

But there was one picture of a naked woman that he looked at for quite a while because she looked a lot like Miss Trixie. She had the same kind of real black hair and the same shaped face and her breasts were shaped almost exactly the way he remembered Miss Trixie's were. He thought that was the prettiest picture in the book and he looked at it for a long time pretending it really was Miss Trixie and he thought that maybe if he ever got any money, any folding money, she wouldn't charge him so much to try some of those things because now he already knew what to do, she wouldn't have to show him.

When he left he put the books back very carefully in the compartment where he'd found them. He knew that he'd like to look at those books again sometime, the ones that had pictures in them, and if Mr. Evans found out Sammy had looked at them he might tell Sammy not to look at them again, but if Mr. Evans didn't know he couldn't tell Sammy not to.

Sammy was glad, when he finally went to the sleeping top, to find that Jesse was sound asleep and snoring. He got under the covers very quietly and carefully so Jesse wouldn't wake up, and Jesse didn't.

CHAPTER SEVEN

Dr. Magus awoke to misery and the sound of rain on canvas. His first coherent thought was of wind and of whether he'd better get out and double-stake or grapevine, but the canvas sidewalls of the mitt camp hung limp and lifeless and there was no sound of stakes being driven elsewhere on the lot. His watch told him it was ten o'clock in the morning and his aching head told him there was no use in trying to go back to sleep.

Slowly his mind began to work through the fog, to pick up the threads of living. I am Dr. Magus, mentalist, working my own mitt camp. It is Wednesday. Wednesday of the second to last week of the season. Now in Bloomfield. One more week after this one. Something important happened yesterday. What? Oh, yes, Mack Irby was killed, only it was the night before last instead of yesterday. And Maybelle spent the rest of the night with me. Rain sounds like an all-day rain. Mud. Not much chance we'll open today. But I'd better get up. This hangover and headache are hell and won't start to go away until I make myself get up and force myself to take a drink of dog hair and to eat some breakfast. My God, did I leave myself a drink?

Laboriously and painfully he lifted his head and looked around. The whisky bottle stood on the footlocker. No cap on it but there was half an inch of whisky still in it. Groaning, he threw back the covers and crawled the length of them until he could reach the bottle. He downed the drink. It was horrible tasting and for a full minute he wasn't sure whether it was going to stay down but it did.

By the time he was sure of that he was shivering, for he was wearing only shorts and the air was cool. He pulled on clothes, dug out a hat, slicker and galoshes from the foot locker, and went to the chow top for eggs and coffee to make him feel human again. It helped, but not much. He'd have to cut down on his drinking, he decided. Almost every night this season he'd gone to sleep either drunk or not too far from it. Almost every night? He tried to think of one single night when he hadn't had at least a few drinks, and he couldn't. That much drinking couldn't be good for him. At that rate, he'd never live to see sixty. But why the hell did he want to see sixty? What had sixty ever done for him?

Gloomy morning. He looked around the chow top for someone to talk to. But there were only four others there. The Quintanas but with Leon looking so sullen it was obviously not a good idea even to say hello to him. And Dr. Magus knew better than even to look at the wife of so psychopathically jealous a man as Leon; he was really over the borderline. The other two people were Barney King and Maybelle. But they were sitting together and seemed engrossed in one another and he didn't feel he should butt in. He slogged through mud and rain back to the mitt camp. Days like this he wondered why he bothered to exist at all.

And when he felt that way there was only one answer.

He slogged through mud again—the rain was slackening—over to Pop Wilson's trailer. Pop ran a little private liquor store, strictly for the carneys because he didn't bother about a license. His main stock was smoke, in unlabeled pint bottles, and it was powerful stuff. But for those who were finicky, he also kept on hand—at slightly more than regular prices, since he had to buy it retail himself—a case or two of standard brand whisky. Dr. Magus had drunk the smoke often enough but today he didn't feel up to it. He felt finicky. He bought a fifth of the finest and oldest whisky Pop had, Seagram's Seven.

Back in the mitt camp he had himself a drink of it and this time, with a breakfast under his belt, it tasted all right. And it took away the cobwebs and he sighed with contentment and lay down again with his hands clasped behind his head, staring up at the canvas top.

What was it, he wondered, that had bothered him about Mack Irby? Certainly it wasn't surprising that he'd been killed and rolled when it had been all over the lot that he was coming back from the hospital loaded with dough from an insurance settlement. Even if whoever had killed him had guessed that the bulk of it would be either in non-negotiable form such as traveler's checks or stashed away somewhere, he'd know Irby would probably carry a fair amount in cash too, as he had. Unless he was pretty stupid the killer could hardly have expected a bigger cash windfall than he got, although he could have hoped the whole thing might be in cash. There were some plenty tough boys on the lot, particularly among the rideboys and the roustabouts; no doubt any one of several of them would gladly have knocked Irby in the head for something over two hundred dollars.

So there wasn't anything mysterious about Irby's being killed. Money had to be the motive, because Dr. Magus felt pretty sure that Irby hadn't had any enemies among the carneys. He'd been a pretty tough boy himself and he hadn't made friends easily but he'd minded his own business and hadn't antagonized anyone either. It couldn't be over a woman. He'd gone straight to Maybelle, and Maybelle had been playing the field since Charlie Flack's death; nobody had any proprietary interest in her now, or had had since Charlie Flack. If Charlie was still alive and Irby had— but Charlie wasn't alive so why consider that?

No, Irby had been killed for the money he had on him.

Then what bothered him about it?

• • •

He decided that it must have been the way Mack Irby had acted that night when he'd dropped into the mitt camp. He'd acted naturally at first. But then he'd called the shot on where Irby was heading and whom he was going to see there, Maybelle. Just a good guess based on observation; back when Maybelle had been Charlie Flack's woman he'd noticed, a few times, the way Irby had looked at her. It was easy to guess that, after seven weeks' forced continence in a hospital a woman would be Irby's first thought and that, now that Charlie wasn't in the way, the woman would be Maybelle.

But a mentalist trains himself to watch reactions. It's his stock in trade in giving readings and he comes to do it subconsciously even when he isn't working.

And Mack Irby had reacted big, just a few seconds after that prediction. Fear. Naked fear and a sudden hurry to get the hell away from there. His story that he had to see someone else first before he looked up Maybelle had been strictly from a sudden rush to leave.

Could it have had anything to do with Maybelle herself? Not any way that Dr. Magus could see. And certainly it hadn't been Mack's conscience because he was doing some posthumous poaching on Charlie's preserve. Mack and Charlie hadn't been that close, and besides seven weeks is a long time. Even Charlie wouldn't expect Maybelle to be faithful to him after he was dead and buried.

And anyway, that reaction had been more than surprise or conscience. A man who's told fortunes for twenty-two years gets to know facial expressions and muscular reactions, gets to know them so well he can't be fooled on them, even the minor ones. Without being able to read emotions from physical reactions, he couldn't possibly give a mark a cold reading and make it good.

Fear. That had been Mack Irby's reaction.

It certainly hadn't been physical fear, no possible reason for it. So it could mean only one thing. That lucky shot had made Mack Irby suddenly afraid that Dr. Magus could read his mind, and there was something in his mind he was desperately afraid to have read.

• • •

Dr. Magus had seen that reaction before, quite a few times, in his years as a mentalist. Make a lucky hit on some statement to a man who has an important guilty secret, and you can watch it dawn on him that maybe you really can either read his mind or discover things about him clairvoyantly—doesn't matter which way he figures it—and he starts to sweat. You can almost smell his fear. Dr. Magus remembered one time, fifteen maybe twenty years ago in Akron, when he'd been giving a reading to a mark, an Italian, and he'd made some statement about the mark's past, he didn't even remember what it had been, but he'd seen and felt that sudden fear and then there'd been a short-barrelled little .32 revolver aiming across the little table between them and the mark was saying, "You know too goddam much. Maybe I better—" But before Dr. Magus could even start fast-talking his way out of it, the mark stood up, jammed the gun back in his pocket and rushed out of the mitt camp as though his tail was on fire. It had scared the devil out of Dr. Magus and for a while after that he gave pretty poor readings, sticking to broad generalizations, to avoid lucky hits. He still did that whenever his instincts told him that the mark across the table from him could be a dangerous criminal.

But he'd never thought of Mack Irby as a dangerous criminal. There'd been larceny in his soul, sure, but almost all carneys have that.

Nevertheless Mack Irby had had a guilty secret and a damned important one. It could hardly be a killing, unless it was a very old one or had happened between seasons, during the winter Irby had been with the Wiggins & Braddock shows for three—no, four seasons now and there hadn't been a killing with the carney—except one that had happened in a knife fight between two jigs—in that length of time.

Except Charlie Flack. For a moment he toyed with the possibility that Mack Irby had somehow engineered that auto accident and had killed Charlie so he could get Maybelle. But he couldn't have; the details of the accident had been clear and there'd been witnesses. The other driver had been speeding and on the wrong side of the road and, if Dr. Magus remembered rightly, had been drunk besides. If there'd been anything off-beat about that accident the insurance company would never have made so quick a settlement with Irby. And besides, Irby himself could all too easily have been killed; he wouldn't have taken so wild a gamble that he'd survive and Flack wouldn't. Usually, the seat beside the driver is more dangerous in a smashup than the driver's seat; it just happened that Irby had been lucky and Flack hadn't. So that idea was out completely.

But what then? No kind of petty larceny would get a reaction like that from a man as tough as Mack Irby. If it wasn't a killing it would have to be something big, something that involved real money, like a payroll robbery or a bank robbery.

And didn't he, now that he thought of it, remember reading in the newspaper of some town they'd been playing two or three months ago about a bank robbery in some town nearby? Two men, or had it been three, getting away with quite a wad of cash?

He tried to pin down the memory, and couldn't. He read so many newspapers, always the local papers of the town they were playing or going to play next. Surprising how many helpful little items a mentalist can find in a local paper.

But he hadn't thought of Charlie or Mack in connection with the robbery at that time. If they'd been away from the lot that day somebody with the carney would have known they were gone and might have connected . . . No, carneys don't read newspapers. Billboard and Variety yes, but not newspapers.

Bank robbery?

Mack Irby, tough though he had been, just couldn't have been in that kind of a league.

Wait a minute.

Charlie Flack could have pitched in that kind of a league. He remembered now that early in the season when Charlie had joined the carney, he'd guessed Charlie to be something more important than he seemed to be. There'd been something about him, a hard wariness in his eyes, a tenseness in his body, that had said this man is dangerous. Charlie had never come for a reading but if he had he'd have got the broad generalization treatment.

And Charlie hadn't really been a carney, although he'd known some of the ropes and some of the lingo. As though maybe Maybelle had coached him. Not that he hadn't fitted beautifully into the job Maybelle had got him with the model show, as inside man. A bouncer's job, really, in there to watch that none of the marks got out of line and tried to go over or under the rope that held them back a safe distance from the stage on which the girls posed. Things like marks getting past that rope could lead to a clem that would wreck the show, maybe the whole carney if it spread. And a clem can spread like a flash fire and be just as destructive. So Charlie's had been an important job and he'd handled it perfectly. Despite the fact that he hadn't been a big man he'd been one who could say, "Back there, you," quietly but in a voice that would get quick and positive results with the toughest or the drunkest marks.

What had Charlie been before he'd joined the carney? Dr. Magus remembered his first guess—that Charlie was a red hot, a moderately big time gangster or robber, either on the lam or holing in with the carney between jobs.

And he and Mack Irby had become close friends.

So even though Irby had been small time up to then, Charlie Flack, with the guts and the experience Irby lacked, could have taken him in on something big. A jackal would not be afraid to help pull down big game if he had a lion to lead him.

Dr. Magus had another drink, but a short one. He might be on the verge of figuring out something and he wanted to get just a slight edge and hold it. His mind worked best that way.

Or, he wondered, was he kidding himself, reading more into Irby's reactions Monday night than there had been?

Well, there was one person who could confirm part of his guess. Maybelle had known Charlie Flack before he'd joined up; it was probably because of her he'd come here, or at any rate she was the reason he'd chosen this particular carnival. She'd know something at least about what he had been. She might even know whether he and Irby had pulled a job together, although he doubted that.

It would be easy to get out of her whatever she knew and she wouldn't even suspect he was doing it. Maybelle believed in fortune telling and had told him Monday night that she'd like to have him give her a reading sometime. He could look her up now on the excuse of wanting to compare notes on how the police lieutenant had taken their story. And once they'd finished that topic she might suggest the reading herself. If she didn't he could easily enough lead her into it in such a way she'd still think it was her own idea and never in a thousand years suspect him of wanting to get rather than to give information.

He hated the thought of having to go out again in the rain, a steady drizzle now, and the mud. But he sighed and again donned the galoshes and the slicker.

He stepped out, deciding to start his search at the chow top since she'd been there half an hour before and might still be there. But luck was with him and he didn't have to search after all. Sammy was going by. He called and Sammy came over.

"Sammy, do you know Maybelle?"

"Yes, Mr. Magus."

"Will you see if you can find her anywhere around the lot and tell her I said to ask her if she'd drop in the mitt camp as soon as she's free and has time? Look in the chow top first." He dug a quarter out of his pocket and flipped it to Sammy.

Sammy caught it and smiled. A nice smile Sammy had.

"Sure, Mr. Magus, I'll find her. And tell her you want to see her."

"When she's got time, Sammy. Don't make it sound like an emergency."

"Yes, Mr. Magus. Say, will you tell my fortune sometime?"

Dr. Magus laughed. "I'll tell it right now. You're going to get rich, Sammy."

"Gee. You mean paper money, folding money?"

"Lots of it, Sammy."

"When, Mr. Magus? Soon?"

"Maybe sooner than you think, Sammy. Run along now and find Maybelle before you forget what to tell her."

CHAPTER EIGHT

The murderer had not slept well. Not nearly so well as he had slept Monday night after killing Mack Irby.

And in the long hours of last night he had come to the reluctant decision that Dolly Quintana was too dangerous to him to be allowed to live. Rather, it was not Dolly herself who was dangerous—he felt full and complete confidence that she would never give him away, probably would not have even if he had not given her money—but it was the explosive situation caused by Dolly's fear of Leon and Leon's completely psychopathic attitude toward Dolly.

He saw now that having given Dolly the money had been a mistake. Whether she used it in an attempt to escape or not, the fact that he had given her that money was a greater danger to him than the fact that she could connect him with murder. If she fled, Quintana would pursue and if he found and caught her the truth would come out. As it would if she stayed and Quintana found the money in her possession. In either case he'd force her to tell where she had obtained the money. He'd believe her as to where she got it, but never as to why. He was too crazy for that. He'd come with knives. And even if he managed to get Quintana first in self defense, the story would come out as to where Dolly had got it and all his careful planning would have been for nothing.

He felt pretty sure now that Dolly wasn't going to run. If she hadn't, up to now, it meant she didn't have the courage to do it. But he was glad now that she hadn't. Because even if she got away clean, if Quintana never caught her, there'd always be the chance that she'd—well, she herself didn't have the courage to try blackmail but suppose she took up with a man who did have the courage, and confided in him? Or for all he knew Dolly might talk in her sleep or in her cups. Always the chance, even the thousandth chance, that something would happen. Dolly knew that he had killed Mack Irby and as long as Dolly lived he'd never feel completely secure.

Dolly must die. And quickly, for not only was the end of the season only ten days or so away but there was always the chance that she would gather what shreds of courage she had and run away, beyond his reach.

Tonight, if possible.

And he worked out a method that seemed foolproof. He knew for sure that Joe Linder, the talker for the freak show, wanted Dolly. And he had a pretty good hunch that Dolly would go for Linder—under the right circumstances. Today, somehow, he'd verify those two things and if they checked, Dolly would die all right. Joe Linder would die with her and that was too bad but it couldn't be helped. For that matter he liked Dolly too, but when your own life is at stake—not to mention the money—you can't afford to be merciful, can you? Your own safety comes first.

Conning Joe Linder came first and he might as well get that over with right away because if Joe didn't fall for it, he'd have to make other plans, and damned quickly.

Maybe, if Joe really went for it, he could use Joe to get Quintana out of the way so he'd have a really good and safe chance to talk to Dolly. Linder and Quintana both worked for the same show and maybe Linder could think of some excuse to get Quintana to go into town with him. That would be perfect. If Quintana was safely off the lot he could even sit at the same table as Dolly in the cookhouse and talk to her face to face, convincingly. Nobody but Quintana would think anything of them sitting and talking together.

He left his trailer, being careful to lock the door behind him as always now, and waded through mud and water to Joe Linder's living top.

Joe was there, and Joe listened and was pathetically grateful for what he offered to do for him. And Joe said he was sure he could get Quintana into town with him.

The first step of Operation Dolly was successful.

CHAPTER NINE

Maybelle Seeley said, "Thanks, Sammy." She gave him a quarter on the off chance that Doc hadn't paid him to look for her. If he had, it didn't matter. And she was glad Doc wanted to see her because she'd been intending to look him up later in the day anyway to ask him for that reading he'd promised to give her. His sending for her made it easier to ask, or maybe even the reading was what he had in mind when he'd sent the message.

On second thought, though, she hoped it wasn't that. Because it just might mean that he'd already cast a horoscope for her—he'd asked her birth date so he could have—and had found something bad or dangerous coming that he wanted to warn her about. If everything had been all right why would he have sent for her? Or he could have seen something in his crystal he thought he should tell her about. Or maybe he'd used numerology with her name, but she hoped not because it wasn't her real name, of course, and that would make it wrong. Or would it, since it was the name she used all the time? It was her stage name, kind of, and she'd read that movie stars consulted numerologists before they picked out the names they used in the movies, so it must be that a stage name counted. Her right name was Elsie Grabow, or it had been until she'd married that Dick Potter when she was seventeen but that had lasted less than a year before they'd broken up and she didn't know now if he was alive or dead or had maybe divorced her. But she hadn't thought much of either Elsie Grabow or Elsie Potter as a name so when she'd first got into show business, a pony in a burlesque road show, she'd picked a better one. She'd seen the name Mabel Seeley on a book and had liked it but had made it even better by changing it to Maybelle.

And she was still worried about Monday night and maybe the cops still finding out she'd been with Mack and making trouble for her. She hoped he didn't have any bad news about that. But it couldn't be that. The cops would have picked her up before this if they hadn't believed her.

She'd been drying her feet when Sammy had found her, having just come in out of the rain and having been foolish enough to wear ordinary shoes that were now coated with mud an inch thick. This time she put on what she should have worn before, rubber boots, and put on her slicker again. Out into the mud that was getting almost ankle deep in places now. But the rain had almost stopped.

She thought about what a surprise Doc had been Monday night. She supposed that at his age—he must be in his fifties—he didn't want a woman too often but when he did, wow. And yet how gentle and considerate he'd been, how different from Charlie and Mack and Dick and almost all of the other men she'd known. They all thought only about their own fun and didn't give a damn about the woman's part of it. Well, she'd tried to give him value for the alibi he was giving her and she knew she had, but the surprising thing was how much she herself had enjoyed it, even after those couple hours with Mack. Or maybe, by contrast, because of them.

Outside the mitt camp she called out, "Doc, you decent?" and he called back, "Not very. But come in, Maybelle." He'd been kidding, though; he was fully dressed, although he hadn't rolled up his bedding yet and was lying on it. But he sat up as she came in.

"Hi, Doc," she said. "Sammy said you wanted to see me."

"At least to see you, my dear."

Maybelle took off her slicker and hung it on the center-pole, stepped barefoot out of the boots. "Will you have time to give me that reading today, Doc? Or was that what you sent for me for?"

"It wasn't, but I'll gladly do it after we compare notes on our interviews with the police. That was what I had in mind. But before either, the amenities."

"The what?" And then Maybelle saw he was holding out a bottle of whisky to her. "Well, it's pretty early in the afternoon but all right, a short one."

She tilted the bottle briefly and handed it back. "Maybelle, was it a Lieutenant Showalter who talked to you?"

"I didn't get his name, Doc. Big guy, plain clothes, dark gray suit, and he had a mole on his cheek."

"That's the one. When did he talk to you?"

"A little before ten o'clock, I think it was."

"Just before he came here. And he hasn't returned, hasn't talked to you again a second time?"

Maybelle shook her head.

"Good. Then I'm sure you've got nothing to worry about. I think I sold him on the idea that Mack could have been alone in that sleeping top after all. At any rate, if he suspected you he'd have been back for a second round of questioning after he talked to me. If he hasn't by now, I think you're safe. If he does, just stick to what you told him the first time and don't let him get you mixed up."

"Sure, Doc."

"Even if he says he now has someone who saw you go to that sleeping top. He'd probably be bluffing just to see if he could get you to change your story. But even if he isn't bluffing, even if he confronts you with a witness who really did see you, stick to your story. It'll be his word against yours—and yours is supported by mine, such as it is."

"Don't worry, Doc, I'll stick to that story whatever happens. If I changed it now I'd get you in trouble too."

"You are a good girl, Maybelle. Ready now for the reading or will you have another drink first?"

"Let's save the drink till after; I'll have one with you then. Are you going to run the cards for me?"

Dr. Magus stood up. "Let's sit across from one another here, my dear, at the table. And I would rather use the crystal than the cards. Palmistry and cards, Maybelle, are good for reading the future in a general sort of way. But for an answer to a specific question, always the crystal. Sometimes, my dear, I almost believe in the crystal myself, and think that I see things in it and that they are not purely my imagination."

Maybelle laughed. "You're kidding me, Doc. Sure, the crystal's fine if you'd rather use it But what made you think I had a special question? I haven't."

"But you have, whether or not you thought of it in connection with this reading. You want to know, do you not, whether the police will continue to believe your story of Monday night or whether trouble may still come to you from it?"

"Sure Doc, but you said—oh, I see what you mean. You said you thought I was safe. But with the crystal you can find out for sure?" Doc was smart. She had had a special question and hadn't even realized it until he'd told her.

"I hope the crystal will tell me, Maybelle. I'll try. But I'm going to be honest with you; this will be a genuine reading or none. If I can see nothing in the crystal for you we'll pass it up and I'll run the cards. No, please don't light a cigarette. I want you to sit absolutely quiet."

His eyes dropped from hers to the crystal and she watched him stare into it, completely motionless. And she sat motionless herself so as not to distract him, so motionless that some of her muscles began to hurt a little. And she began to get scared a little. It was spooky the way he sat there so still and for so long. It must be five minutes at least and maybe ten. What if he was seeing something awful in there, her dying maybe, or being injured or going to jail for something she didn't do?

Then he spoke, his voice low. "I am seeing, Maybelle. But I am seeing things in your past life, not in your future. I shall tell you what I see and then perhaps those things will go away and I shall be able to see ahead. I see deep trouble that you have been in, and always because of a man who was a criminal. When you did something yourself that got you in trouble with the law, it was always because of the influence of a man who was evil."

It was so true that she clenched her hands tightly. Yet she had to protest. "Doc, Dick wasn't really—"

"Evil was too strong a word, Maybelle. But he was bad and he was bad for you. It has been your misfortune to be attracted to men like that. Dick was a long time ago. But there were others and recently there was Charlie. He was bad too."

"He'd been a criminal, Doc. But he was going straight. You know that. He was doing good on his job."

"Think, Maybelle, of how he happened to come here."

"He was hot, Doc, yes, they were looking for him for a job in—he's dead now, so it don't matter I guess what I say—in Kansas, a bank job, and they'd killed a cashier so the heat was on plenty and they hadn't even got any money out of it, just peanuts. But Charlie swore to me that that had cured him and he was going straight and that's why I got him the carney job. I was with him for a while last winter but when I found out what he was I told him I was off him, I couldn't take it living with a man who did things that dangerous and—"

"And you left him and came with the carney. But you believed him when he came here later and told you he was changed. And you shouldn't have, Maybelle."

"Doc, you mean he was lying to me?"

"Lying to you and lying low, Maybelle. Think, think hard, and see it for yourself."

"You mean—damn you, Doc, I tried not to see it. Not that it matters now, but it did then. I think he was planning something, maybe Mack with him. That week in Glenrock just before the accident, it rained a lot that week, remember, we played only I think three days out of the week, and two of the days we didn't play Charlie was gone all day and then one day Charlie and Mack were both gone all day, that was Thursday I think, the day before he got killed. Doc, did they pull a job or were they just still casing one?"

"You tried hard not to see, didn't you, Maybelle?"

"I—I guess I did. They were tense, keyed up. I guess I knew they were going to do something and tried not to see. Did they do it, Doc?"

"I can't—the crystal doesn't show because it's you, things that happened to you, that I'm seeing there, Maybelle. Charlie's lying to you, his still being a criminal and your knowing it and still loving him, that is here because it affected you. But not—" He looked up at her. "But Maybelle, you ought to be able to answer that yourself. Think back about Monday night, the time you spent with Mack."

"You mean I should be able to tell from the way he acted whether or not they'd already—I—I don't know, Doc. We didn't talk much, I guess, in those two hours. He did say he wanted me to go somewhere with him for the winter and that he had a big stake, but he must have meant just that money from the insurance. And he acted—well, kind of like he was tight inside and happy as hell at the same time, but I thought that was natural, just getting back from the hospital and everything."

"Of course it was, Maybelle. Yes, I imagine the accident stopped them in whatever they planned to do." He looked down again at the crystal. "It's changing now. Yes, the shadows of the past are dispersing and I am seeing—" He looked long and in silence again. Then he sighed deeply and as though with relief.

"The future is good for you, Maybelle. I see no trouble. And yes, I can definitely tell you no more will come of your questioning by the police about Monday night."

"Gee, thanks, Doc."

"There is a good life ahead for you. But there is a warning. Beware not only of breaking the law yourself—in serious ways—but of loving any man who does."

He pushed the crystal aside and sighed even more deeply. He got up and brought back the bottle. "And since the word was good, my dear, a drink to celebrate?"

She drank, a bit more deeply this time, and handed the bottle back. "Thanks, Doc, thanks a million. I guess I just realized how much I still was worried about Monday night and the cops and all. But I'm not any more."

She leaned forward and put her hand on his. "And listen, Doc, any time you want to give me another alibi like you did Monday night just say the word."

Dr. Magus smiled. "Thank you, my dear. I will say the word because I know the word, the perfect word, the word that ends unnecessary words. The word is Now."

CHAPTER TEN

By three o'clock the rain had completely stopped. The Murderer leaned against the bally platform of the freak show and watched the cat men putting shavings on the midway. He'd been here half an hour now, since he'd seen Quintana and Linder leave the lot together. He hoped Dolly would come out of her own accord so he could talk to her without having to go in looking for her. But if she didn't come out within a few minutes he'd go on in the freak show top.

He saw Wiggins, the owner, standing over by the ferris wheel watching the cat men too. He strolled over.

Wiggins saw him coming and nodded. Wiggins, he saw, had mud splashes on his suit and his shoes and the cuffs of his trousers were caked with it. But it didn't make him look much sloppier than usual. Wiggy was fat and always looked sloppy; expensive tailor-made suits looked on him as though they'd been bought used at a hock shop; his necktie was always crooked and his beard so heavy that he looked as though he needed a shave even when he'd just had one. You'd never have guessed, to look at him, that he owned and ran a carnival and cleared fifty or sixty thousand dollars a season on it.

Right now Wiggins looked more like a roustabout, the man joining him thought.

"Think tonight'll be okay, Wiggy?" he asked.

"Weather bureau says so; I phoned them."

"Swell. We might get a good play this evening if they're right. The murder got us publicity and a lot of people are going to be coming out on account of it."

"I imagine we got most of that trade last night."

"I doubt it. There's only an evening paper here so most people read about it yesterday evening and too late to make up their minds to come out."

"Hope you're right. If so, maybe we should have murders oftener."

He chuckled. "We should at that. Well, cheer up, maybe we will."

"Maybe we should put one on as a free act instead of the tank dive. Only—seriously—by God, if there is another killing. I hope the son of a bitch gets caught."

"Why?"

"Cop trouble. Another unsolved one and they might slough us. Damn if I didn't have trouble yesterday talking them out of coming out with a search warrant for the whole lot."

A chill went down The Murderer's spine. He hadn't thought of that possibility, and it would have been a rough break if it had happened. Maybe he should get that suitcase out of the trailer and off the lot.

He asked, "How'd you talk them out of it?"

"Convinced 'em it wouldn't do 'em any good. And it wouldn't have. All that was taken off Irby was cash and they couldn't identify it if they found it. I told 'em about weasel sacks and winter money and that they'd find plenty of dough stashed away in amounts over the two hundred thirty bucks or so they figured Irby had and so what?"

"Yeah. The killer wouldn't be dumb enough to keep it separate; he'd add it to whatever roll he already had. So even knowing the exact amount wouldn't help them."

The Murderer thought, well, after tonight if everything goes all right they'll find the money in Dolly's stuff and it will be the exact amount because she didn't have any to add it to. And they'd think they had Irby's murder solved. He chuckled a little about how neatly they'd be fooled and Wiggins looked at him so he had to say something to explain his amusement.

He said, "Just thinking about something that happened last night. When I got back to my trailer after we closed I found I'd left the light on and the door unlocked. I don't ever do that but this time when I'd left earlier I thought I was going back right away and something came up and I didn't, and forgot. But you remember that little collection of pornography I showed you once?"

"Sure."

"Well, some magazines I had in a cabinet were out on the table so I knew somebody'd been there—and who it was. That halfwit kid, Sammy. Jesse's punk. He used to come and ask to look at pictures and I'd let him. Well, then after I put the magazines back I saw the pornography books weren't in the same order— he'd been looking at them too."

"End of story?" Wiggins looked at him. "What's funny about that?"

"Guess you'd have to know Sammy to see what's funny about it. You see, Sammy doesn't know what women are for—or didn't until he looked at the pictures in those books. He got news last night. Wonder if he's going to start giving Jesse trouble now."

Wiggins said, "Oh. Well, I hope he does. None of my business, but that's something I don't like. Why doesn't Rau get himself a broad?"

He shrugged. "Some guys are that way, that's all. In Sammy's case I'd say it's a break for him Jesse's like that; who'd watch out for him if Jesse didn't take care of him? He'd have to go to a nuthouse or starve to death."

Wiggins just grunted. Then he said, "I better phone and see what's holding up that other load of shavings." And headed for the office wagon.

The Murderer had watched the freak show top all the while he'd been talking. I'll give her another few minutes, he decided.

In telling Wiggins about last night he'd left out one little thing. The fact that he'd damn near had heart failure when he'd found he'd left his trailer unlocked and that somebody had been there. He'd had trouble breathing until he'd got that suitcase out from under the bed, unlocked it and checked its contents. It was only later, when he realized who'd been there and why and had found the pornography books in a different order, that it had seemed funny to him. And he still didn't understand how he could possibly have been so stupid and careless as to have forgotten even for a moment, let alone most of the evening, that his trailer was unlocked.

He glanced at his watch. Three-fifteen. And just as he was deciding to go in after Dolly Quintana she came out. She was alone and heading toward the chow top. He cut across the midway so he'd intercept her. He said, "Hi, Dolly," and then under his breath as they passed. "Something to tell you. Sit alone. Join you in a minute."

He kept on walking into the penny arcade, which was the direction his course of interception had taken him, and stopped inside to talk to Jay Klein, who was restocking the two machines that dispensed postcard pictures of movie stars. Then he went to the chow top. Dolly was sitting alone and at an isolated table; whatever she'd ordered was already on the table in front of her so rather than have to be interrupted to have his order taken and brought to him, he got a cup of coffee at the counter and strolled over with it. He sat down across from Dolly.

He said, "Don't be scared, Dolly. Leon went into town with Joe Linder. He won't be back for a while yet and nobody's going to tell him I sat down across the table from you. Everybody with the carney, Dolly, dislikes Leon and feels sorry for you."

"I—I hope you're right. But if he ever—"

"Don't let's waste time talking about Leon. Let's talk about you. You're afraid to run away from him, aren't you? Now, now, don't get a look like that on your face, honey. We're just talking about the weather if anybody should look this way. Act casual."

"I'll try." She took a deep breath. "Yes, I guess I'm afraid to run away. You don't know how—"

"Let me do the talking. Pretend you're eating while you listen. Dolly, I know somebody who wants to help you. With his help you can get away and Leon'll never find you. This guy is in love with you, Dolly."

She stared at him across the table, her fork motionless halfway from the plate to her lips.

"Joe Linder," he said. "He loves you. He wants to help you get away. But he'd stay here till the end of the season so Leon'd just think you went away alone. Then he'd join you—and protect you."

"Joe Linder wants to do that?" Dolly's voice was wondering. "But why? He hasn't ever even—"

"Why hasn't he ever said anything to you or made passes? Because he didn't know you wanted to leave Leon. And if he even acted nice to you he knew Leon would take it out on you, beat the hell out of you. Will you let Joe?"

She drew in her breath sharply. On the way out it said, "Oh, my God yes," as though it was one word.

He smiled. But he said, "Damn it, Dolly, act as though we're talking about the weather. Now listen carefully, here's his plan. Joe's brother and sister-in-law got a little farm in northern California. He's going to spend the winter with them. You too. You'll take off tomorrow or the next day—some time when he or I can arrange to get Leon off the lot again—and go there ahead of him. He'll give you a letter to them. And Joe'll still be here after you leave, the last ten days or so of the season, so Leon won't guess any connection between you.

"By next season Leon'll have another woman and have forgotten all about you. I'll watch that and let Joe know. If not, you and Joe can stay out there, tie up with a West Coast carney, until Leon has got over it."

He could hear her breathing. Damn it, he'd better talk fast and get away from her. She was damn near crying.

He said, "Take it easy, honey. Here's the pitch. You and Joe will need a chance to talk this over, tonight. I got something for you here that'll make it safe as houses." He took a quick look around to be sure no one was looking their way and then reached over and put a tiny glass bottle under the edge of her coffee saucer. "Stick that in your purse quick, out of sight."

He waited until she'd done it. "That's some sleeping stuff. Safe but powerful. If he drinks all of that it won't kill him, and if he drinks even a little he'll sleep like a log, not a chance in a thousand of his hearing you leave and come back or waking up while you're gone. He always takes at least a drink or two after the last show, doesn't he?"

She nodded, wide-eyed.

"All you got to do is get this in the bottle he drinks out of, Dolly. And then wait till he's sound asleep—remember this won't put him to sleep. But once he's sawing timber you can count on at least five or six hours before even a bombing raid would wake him up.

"And then you go to Joe's sleeping top; he'll be there waiting for you, don't worry. Then you and him can talk it over, the details. Okay, I'll tell Joe to look for you." He stood up, knowing that he'd said everything that was necessary and that Dolly wouldn't eat or act natural while he was there. He carried his coffee back to the counter and sat down there, his back to Dolly, drank the rest of it and shoved it across to Hank for a refill.

He was just stirring sugar into it when he happened to glance at the entrance. Quintana was coming in. That had been a narrow one! Not that Quintana would really have started anything, with him sitting well across the table from Dolly. But he'd have been suspicious, and therefore surly and nasty, and he'd have taken his suspicions out on Dolly later, maybe even scaring her out of the courage his pep talk had just given her.

But Quintana was in a good mood, smiling. "Good news, Dolly. Chance for you to make a little extra tonight, doubling. Opal ain't here. She thought this morning it would rain all day and we wouldn't open and her folks live a hunnert miles from here so she took off to visit 'em. So you take over on illusions. Rope tie for the bally and Spider Girl inside."

"All right, Leon." The Murderer was glad that Dolly's voice sounded normal. "How much extra do we get?"

"You let me worry about the money. I take care of that, remember. And listen—"

"What, Leon?"

"Joe Linder'll have to show you the gaff on that rope tie trick for the bally, but it's gonna be with me around watching, see? I'll make sure he don't put his goddam hands on you when he ties you. C'mon, get outside the rest of that grub and let's go get that over with right now."

CHAPTER ELEVEN

When Maybelle had left, Dr. Magus dressed again. Regretfully for now, after that unpremeditated and delightful interlude, he felt now that he could sleep a while and sleep soundly. But fortune beckoned. Maybelle's answers to the questions she hadn't even realized he asked her had been everything he hoped. He felt sure now that his hunch had been right.

So this time instead of putting on the rainy day clothes he'd taken off he dressed himself meticulously in his best suit, added spats and a Panama, took a Malacca stick from the foot locker and made his way across newly spread shavings to the nearest street. Dr. Magus did not leave the carnival lot often and when he did he liked to do it in style. Except for somewhat anachronistic spats, you might have taken him for a specialist in some highly remunerative branch of medicine, perhaps a top-flight psychiatrist, or a college president. But the spats, and to a lesser degree the cane, marked him as none of these; no doctor or professor dares dress anachronistically lest his public assume that his ideas date back to the same eras as his dress. Obviously, then, Dr. Magus was a man of means for only the wealthy dare be eccentric and only the eccentric wear spats.

He enjoyed the deference with which he found himself treated at the office of the Bloomfield Sun. He was shown to a table and there was given and left with a bound volume of issues for July 1st to date.

The accident had been late July, and on a Friday. Maybelle had told him both Charlie and Mack had been gone all day the day before that. If they'd pulled a caper, that would probably have been when.

He decided to see first if the accident itself had made the paper here in Bloomfield, a hundred and twenty miles from Glenrock but in the same state. Besides, it would help him verify the date if he could find mention of it.

Nothing in the paper for Saturday, July 30th. Nor for Sunday the 31st. But on the chance that, although the accident had been a bit too far away to rate a separate story, it might be included in a Monday round-up he tried Monday, August 1st, and found it on the front page:

TWELVE IN STATE DIE IN WEEKEND ACCIDENTS

He ran rapidly down the column until he saw the side head: "Two Killed Near Glenrock" and from there he read carefully.

Two men were killed and one injured in a head-on collision three miles east of Glenrock on Highway 42 a few minutes before midnight Friday. George Slater, 40, of Reedsville, driver and sole occupant of one of the cars, was killed instantly. The driver of the other car, Charles Black, 34, died shortly after admittance to Glenrock Memorial Hospital. His companion, Mark Irby, 29, suffered a broken leg, cuts and bruises, but is reported by the same hospital to be out of danger. Both Black and Irby were employees of Wiggins & Braddock Combined Shows, a carnival which played in Glenrock last week.

Nothing there he hadn't known before except the name of the driver of the other car, if that mattered—and even it might be wrong since they got both Charlie's last name and Irby's first incorrect. But at least he had the date for sure. Friday the 29th.

He could work backward from there.

Except that he started with the Friday paper and didn't have to work back. It was there, right on the first page. Just what he was looking for. Just the show he'd come to see.

MASKED DUO ROBS UNION CITY BANK

Union City, (July 28) ENS—Two
armed men held up the First
National Bank of Union City this

afternoon at 2:25 and escaped with
$42,000 in cash.

Both men wore handkerchiefs tied
bandit style over their faces just
below the eyes and wore hats with
brims pulled down. They entered
with drawn guns and ordered four
employees and two customers to lie
flat on the floor. One stood guard
while the other rifled the vault and
the tellers' cash drawers, taking only
cash in the form of bills and stuffing
it in a musette bag.

On leaving the bank they were seen
to drive east toward the downtown
section of Union City in a black or
dark blue Chrysler sedan.

Smart work, Dr. Magus thought. They'd headed into
and not away from the downtown district, where
they'd quickly have lost themselves in traffic. The
Chrysler sedan would have been a stolen car, of course.
Somewhere downtown they'd have abandoned it and
switched to Charlie's old green Chevrolet and from
that moment they'd be safe. With forty-two thousand
lovely dollars, all in cash. Dr. Magus whistled silently
and read on. Carefully.

One of the men was described as medium height,
medium build, brown or black hair, wearing a gray
suit. The other was slightly taller, perhaps twenty
pounds heavier, blond hair, wore a blue suit. Such as
they were, the descriptions fitted. Or were close
enough.

The money had been mostly in old bills of large
denomination. According to the president of the bank,
the reason for this was that the First National Bank of
Union City acted as a clearing house for other banks in
the county which wanted to exchange such bills for

new or smaller ones, and periodically they were sent to the Treasury Department for replacement.

That was all.

It was enough.

• • •

Dr. Magus returned the bound volume to the file clerk with grave thanks and took his departure.

Outside he took a long deep breath. It all fitted too perfectly to be a coincidence. Union City was only about forty miles from Glenrock and they were both on a main highway. It was even closer to Campton, the town they'd played the week before Glenrock. Charlie would have started casing the job from there.

The way Mack Irby had acted Monday evening in the mitt camp. Maybelle's story. This bank robbery committed by two men whose description roughly fitted Charlie and Mack and on the very day when they'd been away from the lot all day.

It had to be. It was.

But Charlie was dead and now Mack was dead too and where was the forty-two thousand dollars?

Was it, could it be, hidden somewhere on the carney lot? Not on the lot itself, of course, because the carney had been in Glenrock when the money was stashed or hidden and the carney was in Bloomfield now. But hidden in something that moved each week with the carney?

When Mack had left the hospital he'd headed back for the carney like a homing pigeon. He had no financial reason for doing so because according to what Barney King had told him Mack hadn't intended to try to make a connection to work for the final two weeks. Of course there was Maybelle. But if Mack had been able to put his hands on that forty-two thousand bucks without coming back to the carney, would he have come back just for Maybelle? Possible, of course, but there are women just as beautiful and even more beautiful in Florida or California or Mexico City or anywhere a man with forty-two thousand dollars—forty-four counting the two grand from the insurance company—could head.

Of course another reason for his coming back could have been to pick up his trunk—and, by the way, who had his trunk now and had it been searched? Surely the police, investigating his murder, would have found out who was holding his effects—probably Burt, because he'd have had them with the unborn show—and would have looked through them. And what had happened to Charlie Flack's effects after the accident?

Dr. Magus realized where he would have to go, and sighed. He'd never before in his life gone to a police station voluntarily. He went to one now.

●　●　●

Lieutenant Showalter was in. He said, "Hi, Doc. What's on your mind?"

"Is there anything new on the Irby matter, Lieutenant?"

"Nope. Why? You found out something?"

"No, I haven't. My question was idle curiosity. But I chanced to be downtown and thought I'd drop in to ask you where Irby's effects are, and, whether any relatives have come forward to claim them."

"Nope, and there won't be. He had no relatives."

"Oh? How can you be certain of that?"

"Traced him back. He carried an Illinois driver's license that gave Shiocton, Pennsylvania, as his birthplace, and the date. So we phoned Shiocton police to check on him. They didn't find a birth certificate but there's a big orphan asylum there and they thought to check with it. He was brought up there, parents unknown, and released when he was sixteen. So anybody'd have a hell of a time claiming relationship."

"Except a wife. He could have married sometime and never have been divorced."

"Yeah, there's that. Why? You know of one or did he ever talk about having been married?"

"No, no, I merely mentioned a possibility. Where are his effects? Do you have them or are they still on the lot?"

"We've got them. No relatives and no will so they belong to the state. That is, they'll be held for a year and then go to the state unless somebody's put in a claim. But don't get any ideas, Doc, about sending someone around claiming to be his wife unless she's got a marriage certificate that will stand checking on."

"Nothing was farther from my mind, Lieutenant. Although it's an idea, if I thought I could get away with it. Two thousand dollars isn't hay."

"A little more than that. Eighteen hundred out of the two thousand that he had in traveler's checks plus nine hundred and fifty that he'd put into postal saving during the three or four months before the accident. The certificates were in his trunk. But what's all this to you, Doc?"

"Nothing at all, as far as the money is concerned. But I'm hoping you found something of mine among his effects, a book. It completely slipped my mind until today, what with the excitement of a murder, but it is a very valuable book and I'd like to have it back."

The lieutenant frowned. "I looked through his stuff and I don't remember any book. What kind was it?"

"A book on astrology, a rare old one printed in England in 1810. I don't know that its monetary value was great—I found it in a used bookstore on Gark Street in Chicago and bought it for a dollar and a half. But it's irreplaceable and there were things in it that I use occasionally. Mack was interested in astrology and had borrowed it a week before the accident. I had in mind to ask him for it as soon as he got back from the hospital but it slipped my mind until today. The book was in English but the title was in Latin—Astra et Homines, stars and men."

"I'm sure now that there wasn't any such book, Doc. I'm sure I'd remember it now that you've described it. A book with a Latin title I know I'd remember. And now that I come to think of it, I know there weren't any books. Some true detective magazines but no books at all."

Dr. Magus looked disappointed. "Is there any chance that it could have been pilfered from the trunk?"

"Not a chance, Doc. There was a watch, a fairly good one, in that trunk, and a few other small but fairly valuable things that a thief would have taken instead of a book. Besides the trunk was locked with a damn good padlock and was packed away under some other stuff in a truck. Your carney owner, Wiggins, was taking care of it until Irby came back for it."

"Wiggins? I'd have thought Burt would have held it for him."

"I wouldn't know about that. We were told Wiggins was holding Irby's trunk and got it from him."

Dr. Magus sighed. "Well, I guess I've lost the book. Unless Irby had loaned it to someone else before the accident. I'll ask around the lot. Thanks a lot, Lieutenant." Curiouser and curiouser, he thought. Why had Burt turned the trunk over to Wiggins instead of keeping it until Irby got back? Of course it could be that Burt was short of packing space after Barney King, who no doubt had a trunk of his own, had come to work for him.

He'd have to ask Wiggins. Would Wiggins be at the lot now or back at his hotel? Wiggins spent plenty of time on the lot but he always stayed at a hotel, the best one in town, ate his meals there and commuted in his car to the carney lot. And it was now six o'clock; Wiggins would quite likely be at the hotel. Let's see, what was the hotel Wiggy was staying at here? He'd heard him mention it. Oh yes, the Carter House. Since he was already on the main drag and near the center of the town he looked down the street and—yes, there was the Carter House sign, only a block away. He walked there and got Wiggins' room on the house phone; Wiggins answered and said come on up.

On the way up in the elevator he decided that the song and dance on the astrology book would work just as well with Wiggins as it had with the lieutenant and that he might as well stick to it. He stuck to it.

"Sorry, Doc," Wiggins said, "but it wasn't in Mack Irby's trunk. I helped the police inventory it, and Charlie Flack's trunk too, the night of the accident."

"You're sure there wasn't a book in either of them?"

"Nary a book, as far as I remember. In either trunk."

"Not that it matters," Dr. Magus said, "but why would the police have opened Mack's trunk? He wasn't dead."

"No, but he was unconscious and they didn't know yet that he wasn't hurt worse than a broken leg. Thought they might as well check to see if he had any relatives who ought to be notified, while they were checking the same deal on Charlie Flack."

"You personally helped them inventory both trunks?"

"Yeah. I happened to be working late with Smitty in the office wagon that night, when they got here, two state cops. I helped 'em locate both trunks—Mack kept his in Burt's unborn show top and Charlie in the model show top—and watched 'em look through. Figured if the boys had any money stashed, no use the cops getting their lousy hands on it."

"Hell, no. They have any?"

"Charlie had about four hundred in his trunk. Mack had some postal savings certificates, but no cash."

Dr. Magus sighed. He was getting good practice in sighing today. He said, "Well, I guess my book is lost. Unless maybe Mack had it lying around loose, not in his trunk. I'll ask Burt if he saw it."

"Hope you find it, Doc. Say, want a lift back to the lot? I just had something to eat and came up here to put on a clean shirt. I'll go back in a few minutes."

Dr. Magus declined, explaining that he had one more but very important thing to do while he was in town and that he'd take the bus or a taxi out later.

And an important thing it was indeed. He hadn't had a drink for four or five hours now and it was high time.

And just look at the extremely interesting things he'd learned this afternoon? He needed a chance to think.

So fifteen minutes later, a lovingly lighted fifty-cent cigar between his fingers, he stood with one foot on polished brass and one elbow on polished mahogany.

"Bushmills Irish, please. A double, over ice."

Dressed as he was and feeling as he felt he could order no less in either quality or quantity.

He smiled at himself in the backbar mirror, and reflected. With forty-two thousand dollars he could drink like this, dress like this, really be what at this moment people took him to be.

Forty-two thousand dollars, and only he even suspected.

Forty-two thousand dollars. No more reading sweaty palms for stupid people.

Forty-two thousand dollars. A bachelor flat. Women when he wanted them, women at least as physically attractive as Maybelle but more intelligent, more polished.

Forty-two thousand dollars. The books and records he had always wanted to own. All the Irish whisky he would ever want—or live—to drink.

Uisgebaugh forever.

If he could answer the forty-two thousand dollar question: Where?

Mack and Charlie had had the money as of Thursday afternoon; they'd done something with it by Friday night, hidden or stashed it so well that it hadn't turned up since.

It definitely had not been in either of their trunks. Fortune had favored him with positive knowledge of that. Both trunks had been searched right after the accident, by cops being watched by carneys. He wouldn't trust either faction alone, but the two together, positively. Neither would dare trust the other, would dare even suggest glomming onto the money and dividing it among them. Nor could they conceivably have missed finding it in the trunks no matter how careless the search. That much money in assorted bills would have quite a bit of bulk.

Or could they have stashed it off the lot?

Pretend to be both of them, he told himself, and talk it over with yourself. Reason the way they'd reason.

"Okay, Mack, we got this dough. But we still got to be careful and lay low like I told you till the season's over, see? If we cut loose sooner somebody'll start wondering why. I don't think we ought even to divvy it till then. Hide it all in one place and there'll be less chance of it being found than if we put it two places."

"Okay, Charlie. But how's about a safe deposit vault? We could take one in both our names and fix it so we both gotta be there to get back into it."

"Use your head, Mack, that'd be a dead giveaway, anywhere within hundreds of miles from here. Every bank around here knows about that robbery by now and we rent a box on terms like that and there'd be cops on our necks before we even got outside. I thought of renting one before, but even that would have been bad—we'd have had to go to it together right after the robbery and put in a package the size of the loot. That and our having it fixed so we could only get into the box together, two of us, would make somebody suspicious sure as hell."

"Well, one of us could rent a box."

"That wouldn't be too risky, Mack. But it sure as hell ain't going to be you. You trust me to do it?"

"Sure I trust you, Charlie. But—hell, I see what you mean. If we can figure a way to hide it right here on the lot where we can both keep an eye on it, kind of— Say, I know a place nobody'd ever find it!"

"Where, Mack?"

Where, Doc?

He looked down into his glass on the bar in front of him but the money wasn't there. Neither was any whisky.

All too well he knew that if he had another now he wouldn't read any mitts tonight. Only a week and a half of the season left now and his winter fund still wasn't what he'd like it to be.

Besides, the show must go on. Or must it? The carney could get along for one evening without a mitt camp. And if he sobered up he'd realize how slim a chance actually he had of getting that money for himself. Whereas if he kept on drinking he could dream about it, even spend it in his imagination. They couldn't take that away from him.

He caught the eye of his reflection in the back bar mirror and it stared at him somberly for a moment and then winked at him. He beckoned to the bartender.

CHAPTER TWELVE

Joe Linder was the best talker on the lot. You have to be the best to hold down the mike for the freak show because that's the biggest show with a carnival, the one with the biggest overhead and the biggest take; you've got to be able to pull them in to talk and grind for a freak show. You've got to have what it takes, and Joe Linder had it. You'd never have thought it to look at him. Smallish, blondish, mild-mannered, if you'd seen him on the street you'd have taken him for the meekest of bookkeepers.

But with a mike in his hand he was different. And now he had a mike in one hand and the stick of the bass drum in the other. He thumped the bass drum.

Get the tip and turn the tip. Boom ta boom boom boom.

"Huh-ry, huh-ry, huh-ry, right this way, just in time for the big FREE show we're going to give you right out on this platform, FREE, it won't cost you a penny to see some of the strangest people in the world. This is the BIG show, the BIG show that gives you fifteen separate wonderful shows inside, EACH one worth the price you see all of them for . . . But you're not going to pay anything, not a cent, to see a few of these strange and gifted people here and now on this platform! It's free, it's FREE, so huh-ry, huh-ry." Boom ta boom boom boom.

Not a big tip and mostly kids, but it was about as big a one as he was going to get right now and if he stalled any longer some of them would start wandering off so he gave the single boom of the drum that was the call to bally and went into his spiel as he heard them coming up on the platform beside him. Dolly first for flash, dressed in spangled trunks and halter. Right after her that son of a bitch husband of hers in a red silk shirt, carrying his throwing knives. Dixie with his rack of eating swords. And Midge—Admiral Tim.

Boom ta boom boom boom.

"Step in closer, folks, right to the edge of the platform. First I want you to meet a little lady who is going to show you that ropes cannot . . ."

Dolly standing against the stocks with her white arms outstretched along the crossbar. He walked over to her with the ropes and tied one wrist to one end of the cross bar, pulling the knot tight—but very careful, under Leon's baleful eye, not to touch her skin—not with his hands, that is; his mind caressed and kissed it. And as he walked past her to tie the other wrist he said, "Huh-ry, huh-ry, huh-ry," very softly under his breath. He knew Dolly heard it and got it by the sudden movement of the throat muscles under her white skin.

" . . . and the little lady, when I give the signal, will step right away from those ropes. Until then, watch her . . ."

That had them hooked; they'd watch her while he sold them on the show, on coming inside the BIG show, they'd feed their damned eyes on the white smoothness of her bare legs and midriff, arms and shoulders, gloat over the contours of that spangled bra and picture the breasts under it. But they could only look and imagine whereas this very night, only a few hours from now—

Another bally and again and the long grind, the BIG show, fifteen different shows all for one low price, come right in, now going on, stay till you've seen a whole show.

But Joe Linder was worried. Why did that one worry have to keep heckling him? Why couldn't he forget it and have only anticipation of the night to come and, if things worked out okay, of the years to come?

It wasn't Leon. Leon was stupid; he'd have no trouble fooling Leon. And he knew a place to take Dolly after the season where Leon would never find them.

It was Evans. Why was he sticking his neck out, arranging this? What did he have to gain? Nothing. It didn't fit his picture of Evans that the guy would—

And then, suddenly it came to him what Evans' motive must be. He wasn't the kind of a guy who did favors, so he wasn't doing Dolly a favor at all. Quintana must have stepped on his toes somehow, and he was doing this to take revenge on Quintana, making him lose Dolly.

That made sense. That fitted. Why hadn't he thought of it sooner?

He could think about Dolly now, and he did.

She'd never sleep with Leon again; he'd made up his mind about that. An hour with her to bind the bargain and then he'd take her to a train tonight, or a bus. Trains at 2:14 and 4:08. A bus at 12:50 and an early morning one at 5:00. He'd see she got on one of those—which direction she started out in didn't matter and by the time Leon woke from drugged sleep she'd be safely out of his reach.

And he'd be back on the lot, alone and asleep in his own top, and Leon wouldn't suspect a thing. Why should he? He'd made a point of doing nothing all season that would make Leon remotely suspect him of being willing to give a right arm to have Dolly.

Leon wouldn't ever find them, either, no matter how long he carried the torch and kept looking. Joe Linder had something up his sleeve on that, something he wasn't telling even Evans, nor Dolly until he had her safely away. Australia. Almost another world, Australia, as remote as the moon or Mars. He had a friend who was there now and who'd been writing wanting him to come. Mice Murdoch, who'd been his buddy for years with the Craft Shows, with a circus in Australia, but he wrote there were good carneys there too and the grift was fine. He'd been thinking about taking Mike up on it anyway and to keep Dolly safe from Leon it would be the smart thing to do.

The long grind, the BIG show, fifteen separate superb acts all for one price, now going on, see the whole show, the strangest people on earth . . .

CHAPTER THIRTEEN

The taxicab let Dr. Magus off at the carnival entrance. The meter showed an even dollar and Dr. Magus munificently tipped the driver another dollar. It startled him into saying thanks, and then, "Say, mister."

Dr. Magus, who had just closed the door, put his head through the front door window opposite the driver. "Yes, my friend?"

"Sure you don't want me to drive you back to town?"

"I am quite sure. May I ask why you make the suggestion?"

"Well, you're a bit polluted, mister. And them carneys are crooks, all of 'em. If you go in there they'll gyp you if they can and roll you if they can't."

Dr. Magus looked at him in shocked wonder. "Are you really certain of that? Are you sure?"

"Sure I'm sure. All the games in there is rigged. Sucker stuff. If you wanta gamble, you oughta go somewhere where they run a straight game."

Dr. Magus's eyes got even wider. "You could take me to such a place?"

"Well, yeah. Not right in Bloomfield, but a few miles out the other side of town."

"Would it have a roulette wheel? I ask because they would not let me play cards, I fear."

"Sure it's got a wheel. But what you mean they wouldn't let you play cards? You been there before?"

"No, no. But someone there would be almost certain to recognize me. I am one of the top—it would be immodest for me to say I am the top—sleight of hand artists in the world. I am especially famous for the Reynaldi sleight with a dollar bill. Here, give me back the one I just gave you for a tip and I'll show you. Thank you, my friend. Now I fold it thus twice, hold it between my thumb and fingers, make a pass so—and it has disappeared."

"Not bad. But look, mister, you want me to take you to the Four Aces or not?"

"Some other time perhaps."

"Okay. Well, give me the buck back"

"That is the second step of the sleight and I am afraid I have not yet perfected it. But thank you just the same." Dr. Magus strode rapidly through the entrance gate before the driver could get out his side of the cab and around it—if he intended to try. Dr. Magus felt fairly sure that he wouldn't; he'd realize by now that his passenger had been a carney and that it wouldn't be healthy to follow him onto the lot to start trouble. As, indeed, it wouldn't have been; there wasn't a carney on the lot who wouldn't have enjoyed helping take that taxi driver apart.

He saw that the midway was jammed and business was good. He threaded his way through the crowd to the mitt camp and let himself in without putting back the outer flaps that would make the joint open for business. He turned on the overhead bulb and put down on the table the cylindrical package he'd carried out from town with him, a bottle of Irish whisky.

He looked at his watch and sighed as he realized that, since it was only ten o'clock, he could and should open for business. With a crowd like that outside he might still take in twenty bucks or so by midnight, maybe thirty or thirty-five if he got a few live ones for five-dollar readings.

But to hell with twenty or even thirty-five bucks.

It was when he was in this exact degree of inebriation that, not often but occasionally, he really saw or thought he saw things in the madball. Like the time when, just about this drunk, he'd been giving a mark a cold reading with the pasteboards but had happened for no reason to glance to one side into the crystal and he'd clearly seen in it the face of a beautiful Negro woman—and had known somehow that it had nothing at all to do with the mark he was reading cards for. And two days later Slim had touted him to make a two-buck bet on a long shot named Black Beauty and suddenly he remembered what he'd seen in the crystal and had surprised the hell out of Slim by giving him twenty bucks to put on the horse. And it had come in at sixteen to one. Slim had gone out to the track with it, luckily, or a bookie would have paid only ten, so Dr. Magus had three hundred bucks profit on his double sawbuck after he'd given Slim forty for the tip and placing the bet. And there'd been the time just last season in Green Bay when he'd been giving a mark a reading with the madball and had seen suddenly and clearly the picture of a car breaking through a railing and going off a bridge. Of course he'd said nothing about it to the mark. The next day he read that a car had gone off a bridge and killed the driver at two o'clock that morning and there'd been a small and blurry picture of the victim; it could have been the man he'd given the reading to. But he didn't investigate to find out if it really was the same man because it had scared him a little. He didn't want to see things like that. Of course those cases and the few others like them could have been coincidence, but it was funny that they happened only at times when he really saw or thought he saw something in the madball.

Well, coincidence or not, tonight while he was in the right shape and the right mood he'd give the madball a chance at the jackpot question, and to hell with business.

But first to relax. He made himself comfortable by getting out of his good clothes and into old ones. And because it had been a full hour since his last drink he unwrapped and opened the bottle of Irish. He had himself a medium sized drink and sat down at the little table and moved the crystal in its stand over in front of him.

He stared into it and concentrated: Where is the money? Will I find it?

From outside the canvas came the carnival sounds, the merry-go-round organ playing Blue Danube, the voices of the talkers, the crowd murmur, the thousand sounds that added up to one single sound as familiar to Dr. Magus as the beating of his own heart. He listened to them deliberately until his conscious mind could hear them no longer, until they were part of the night and one with the night, as silent as the music of the spheres.

There was a sudden bright flash of light in the crystal, then for a brief moment black darkness. Dr. Magus blinked, and again the crystal was as it had been before, reflecting his own distorted face and the interior of the mitt camp curving upon itself like an Einsteinian universe.

Dr. Magus looked around him and upward to see if there really could have been a flash of light anywhere that had reflected itself in the crystal and for a moment almost blinded him. But there was nothing.

He frowned. Had he really seen a flash in the madball or could it have been the sudden twinge of an optic nerve? If he'd really seen it, what could it mean?

Light? The money hidden in the diesel generator truck that made light and power for the carnival? Or in a fuse box somewhere in one of the individual tops or concessions? No, the diesel truck didn't make sense; the electricians, two of them, were working around it half the time. And it would hardly be in a fuse box— too much chance of someone opening it to replace a fuse. Besides—for the first time it occurred to him to wonder just exactly how bulky forty-two thousand dollars, mostly in large bills, would be. Surely bigger than would go in the extra space in an ordinary small fuse box.

Not too big, either, if they'd stuffed it into a musette bag at the bank. If he had the right thing in mind as a musette bag it wouldn't hold over a cubic foot.

Any size he decided, of course, would be a more or less random guess unless he knew the approximate number of bills of each denomination and there wasn't any way he could ask any such intimate questions about that bank robbery without being asked equally intimate and even more embarrassing questions in return. And the police, if anything ever led them to couple the bank robbery and the carnival in their minds, would dig in and figure out the same thing he had.

But with a little thought he could get a rough idea of the size of a package containing forty-two thousand dollars. Of course, in thousand-dollar bills you could carry it in your wallet. And in one-dollar bills you'd have trouble carrying it at all. But it wouldn't be either of those extremes. Thousand-dollar bills exist but aren't often used; there might possibly be a few of them but the bulk of the money would be in hundreds, some fifties, probably lots of twenties and tens, fives—not too many singles or the musette bag wouldn't have held it.

After a while he decided that with any assortment that would be probable he didn't have to consider a package that would be smaller than a cigar box. And that, in considering or looking for a hiding place, only the minimum mattered. All he had to figure out was a hiding place right on the carney lot that would hold a package at least the size of a cigar box. Not necessarily the shape of, but at least the size of. And it would have to be a place which, in any ordinary course of events, wouldn't be looked into during the nine weeks that had remained of the season at the time of the robbery.

Damn it, the very difficulty of thinking of even one such place convinced him that there couldn't be too many such. And, at the same time, made him doubt his first judgment that they'd really hidden it on the lot.

Damn the crystal. If it (or through it God, the devil or his own clairvoyance if any) had tried to tell him something with that flash of light, why hadn't it been clearer about it? Why so cryptic and apparently meaningless a thing as a flash of light?

He pushed it aside, sighing with pleasure at its fiery smoothness. Even if that idea about the money was all wrong it had done one thing for him; it had loosened his financial inhibitions so that for one evening he had been drinking and would continue to drink the whisky he liked best instead of the kind he could best afford. And it had given him amazingly pleasant thoughts and dreams of having an amount of money almost beyond—

The thought hit him suddenly and it was so simple and logical that he wondered why he hadn't thought of it hours ago. Even while he was sober. So logical that it might lead him to the money even if it wasn't with the carnival. True, in that case it might be in a lock box or other place where he couldn't get it himself, but even then there ought to be a sizable reward for telling them how to make recovery of so large a sum of cash.

He'd start tomorrow from the logical place to start.

Glenrock.

He drank a toast to Glenrock.

CHAPTER FOURTEEN

The show was over, the last show of the big show. Behind the canvas partition which Leon always stretched across one corner of the freak show top as soon as the last mark was gone Dolly hurriedly took off the spangled trunks and halter and quickly pulled a gingham dress over her head, not bothering to put on panties and a bra under it. She sighed with relief when she'd successfully made the change before Leon came back to join her; tonight he'd put up the partition and then had gone to see the boss, probably to collect whatever amount was due for her doubling on the illusion acts. That had been a break because it had given her this chance to change out of her show clothes quickly before Leon came back to join her. Had he been here he would have watched her change—and he might have, as he sometimes did, grabbed her and used her then and there, quickly and brutally. That would have been truly horrible tonight, when she was waiting to go to Joe; she'd feel defiled if Leon used her first. It could still happen after they went to bed, but at least one danger point was passed. She hoped he'd drink heavily tonight, even though that meant waiting longer before she could go to Joe, because when Leon drank heavily he was less likely to bother her. Leon was less unpleasant to her, too, when he'd been drinking, although he was always less likely to want her physically then. Sometimes he even got a little sentimental, even told her that he loved her, when he was partly drunk. She'd learned long ago that that was the only time ever to ask him for money for anything she needed, new shoes, a new dress. And if he said okay, he'd remember the next day and give her whatever he'd promised, although grudgingly.

Sometimes when he was a little drunk and was being nice to her, she would almost feel toward him as she once had and want him. But those times he almost never wanted her. He could be kind or he could be sensual but never both things at the same time. It was as though he had to be angry to want her. But drinking made him so different that she had often wished he'd give up knife throwing and do something else because he never threw a knife unless he was completely sober and for that reason never took even a single drink during the day or evening until after the final show. Not that she had any complaint about that, since it was at her that he threw those knives. But she could wish he'd find some other occupation that didn't require his being so cold sober and surly all day and all evening long. But what else could he do? Knife throwing was the only skill he had.

Now, her body safely covered, she pulled back an end of the canvas partition and looked out between it and the sidewall. He was still talking to the boss, clear over on the other side of the top. So it was safe now, if she worked fast, to empty the little bottle of sleeping stuff into—no, it would be too risky now; she couldn't count on time enough to get the bottle out of his trunk and put it back, and he'd be mad as hell if he caught her with his trunk opened, let alone putting something into his whisky. That would have to wait a later chance, after he'd got the bottle out and opened it himself; probably he'd go to the doniker and that would give her lots of time. Even if he just stepped outside under the canvas there'd be time if she had the little bottle ready and the whisky bottle was standing there already opened.

At least she had time now to have the little bottle ready. She got it from her purse and put it in the pocket of the gingham dress, then remembered she hadn't tried the cork and made sure it wasn't too tight to come out easily by taking it out and putting it in again. It was a tiny bottle; it couldn't have held over a teaspoonful of fluid. The fluid in it was clear and transparent, for all the world like plain water. She wondered what it was. But what did the name matter as long as it worked?

She was sitting on her trunk trimming her toenails when Leon came. He stood looking down at her for a minute without saying anything and then he opened his trunk and took the whisky bottle from it, a fifth bottle a little less than half full. He twisted off the cap and drank from it.

She asked, "Can I have one, Leon?" He never offered her a drink but he always gave her one on the rare occasions when she asked for it. She didn't drink much or often; it tended to upset her stomach and she could never get drunk because she'd always get sick first. But tonight she needed at least one drink to quiet her nerves.

He passed her the bottle. "Drink all you want to, Doll. Just leave me a nightcap. I'm going over to the G-top." When the meaning of what he just said sank in, Dolly almost choked over the raw whisky going down her throat. Why tonight of all nights did he want to play poker in the gambling top? True, he played an average of about twice a week and he hadn't played for several nights now; she should have counted on the possibility, even the probability, of it happening. But she'd overlooked it completely. For a moment she almost cried out, "Leon, please don't!" But then she realized she didn't dare; she couldn't give a reason why she didn't want him to play, and she'd never objected before. Most times she'd been really glad to be alone for a while, even though she could never count on being safely alone while he was gone because he usually came back briefly several times on one excuse or another but really to check up on her, to be sure she was still here and alone. If she wanted even to go for a cup of coffee she'd have to go to the G-top first and tell him she'd be in the chow top for a while; and like as not five or twenty minutes later he'd come to the chow top himself presumably to get some coffee too but really to make sure she was there and either alone or in the company of another woman.

But tonight of all nights! He might play all night long if he won and she didn't dare leave here while he played!

She'd have to get word to Joe somehow, at whatever risk; she couldn't bear to think of his waiting for her all night long when she might not be able to come at all.

She said, "Can I have a buck, Leon? I'm getting hungry. Think I'll go over for coffee and a sandwich now." She was thinking fast; a few minutes from now would be the safest time to let Joe know. She could go past his sleeping top between her and the chow top and tell him she probably wouldn't be able to come and if she did it would be awfully late.

Leon took a small roll of bills from his pocket, peeled off the outside one and gave it to her. Then he took another quick drink of the whisky and left, lifting the sidewall of the top and ducking under it.

She stared at the whisky, wondering if she should risk putting the sleeping stuff in it now. Surely she was safe for a few minutes; not until he'd bought chips and played at least a hand or two would he leave the game to check up on her here or at the chow top. She found a tumbler in her trunk and poured into it about two ounces of whisky from the bottle so she could have a couple more drinks herself to help her stay awake and then, listening very carefully for footsteps, she emptied the teaspoonful of clear liquid from the little bottle into the whisky bottle and shook it so it would mix bwell. The bottle was less than a third full now so that would make it fairly strong with the sleeping draught; it would probably work all right on Leon if he took even a couple more drinks out of it after he came back. And if he came back early he might even drink it all before he turned in.

But whether he got back early or not would depend on whether he won or lost. Leon was systematic in his gambling. He always played a certain definite amount—she wasn't sure just how much it was but she thought it was ten dollars—and he never lost more than that in any one game; when it was gone he would quit. But if he won he'd play on till the game broke up and that was seldom before dawn.

So tonight, if he started out losing, he might be back quickly, half an hour or even less, and everything would be all right. But what if he won! She'd have to get word to Joe. And right now, with the game just getting started, would be the least risky time to do it.

She drank half of the whisky she'd poured into the tumbler to give her courage and then stepped into a pair of slippers and went out under the sidewall.

She took a quick look in the direction of the G-top to be sure Leon wasn't coming back and then ran around behind the freak show top and to Joe's place. No light. She called, "Joe," softly and then, when there wasn't any answer, again and more loudly.

He couldn't be there or he'd have heard that second call, He hadn't, of course, expected her this early. After all it was less than half an hour since the last show they'd put on; Joe would figure at least an hour for Leon to go soundly enough to sleep, even if he turned in right away.

She hurried back to the midway and along it to the chow top. Maybe Joe would be there.

But he wasn't. She waved to a few groups at tables but didn't join them. She sat alone at the counter instead. She'd make her sandwich last as long as she could and maybe Joe would come in. Joe or Mr. Evans; either would do because if she could tell Evans he'd get word to Joe. All she had to tell either of them was that Leon was playing poker. From that either of them would know the score—that Leon might come back at any unexpected minute or he might play all night, and that she couldn't take the risk of going to Joe until Leon was back.

She sat so she could watch the door while she ate. If either of them came in she could start out right away, as though she didn't want to finish her sandwich, and could speak those few words as she passed him.

But it was Leon, not Joe or Evans, who came in just as she was finishing her sandwich.

He said, "Doll, I can use a sandwich myself. And since you're here I won't have to wait for it. Will you get me one and bring it to the G-top on your way back?"

"Sure, Leon. A hamburger?"

"Nah, make it a cheese. Easier to eat while I'm playing cards."

"Okay, I'll bring it. How you doing?"

"So-so. Few bucks ahead. Hurry up with it, will you?"

He went out and she ordered a cheese to go. She couldn't sit here now any longer than it would take Hank to make the sandwich; Leon had seen that she'd finished her own meal and would be expecting her right away. Well, making a stop at the gambling top first would make it safer for her to go back by way of Joe's place again and maybe by now he'd be there and she could tell him.

But when she went into the G-top to give Leon his sandwich she saw that everything was all right. Joe Linder was in the poker game too, sitting right next to Leon. He'd been smarter than she because he'd realized Leon might decide to play tonight and had done the smart thing by joining the game himself. If Leon lost he'd know exactly when Leon left and he could leave a few minutes later and be waiting for her. If Leon won and played all night he'd know that too.

And that meant—why, it meant she could go to him no matter how long Leon played, even if he played until five in the morning it would be all right. He'd still take a few drinks out of that bottle, and if he played that long he'd be so dead sleepy that it would probably be safe even if he didn't. Surely once he got to sleep after an all-night session he wouldn't waken for at least a few hours.

She very carefully didn't look at Joe nor he at her while she was in the G-top. She gave Leon his sandwich and hurried out, back to their living quarters behind the canvas partition.

She might as well turn in and pretend to be sleeping when he came back. She turned off the bare bulb that dangled from overhead; there was still plenty of light to see by, coming in over the top of the partition from the high bulb in the middle of the top that was left burning all night. In the relative dimness she slipped the gingham dress over her head and folded it neatly on one corner of her trunk where she could get it easily when the time came. Then, with the slip in which she slept in her hands ready to put on, she looked down at her body, suddenly and pleasantly aware of it, of its nakedness. She saw that it was good, thought of it being caressed and fondled, a source of ecstacy to herself and to another. She dropped the slip onto the trunk and for a moment her hands cupped her breasts and it was as though Joe's hands were there instead of her own.

Then, suddenly realizing that Leon might come back at any moment, she put the slip on quickly. She unrolled the bedding and spread it, got in under the blanket. Before lying down she reached for the tumbler on the corner of the trunk and drank what was left of the whisky she'd poured out for herself. She almost wished now that she'd saved out more before doping the rest. But perhaps it was better that she hadn't. It would be horrible to make herself drunk or sick tonight.

She lay back and closed her eyes, to dream awake, knowing there was no slightest danger of her falling asleep no matter how long the wait.

CHAPTER FIFTEEN

Standing in the dark at the window of his trailer, the window that gave him a full view of Joe Linder's sleeping top, The Murderer sweated.

Something had gone wrong, or was going wrong.

Almost half an hour ago he had seen Dolly go to that top and stop outside, stand there a moment and then hurry on. Wasn't Linder there to answer her call? Or hadn't she called? Had she simply lost her nerve?

The thing had seemed so simple, so foolproof, when he'd planned it, and now he saw chance after chance for something to go wrong. If they weren't both killed, for instance, if one of them was only injured, his part in it would come out in the survivor's story. His acting as intermediary between them in making the assignation, his having given Dolly the little bottle of "sleeping stuff" that could be proved, even from the empty bottle, to be water. He'd have some impossible explaining to do if that happened. And if it was Dolly who survived, the fat would really be in the fire. Once she realized how he'd double-crossed her on the sleeping potion she'd tell them that he'd killed Mack Irby.

He tried to pull his mind back from panic and make it think logically for him. Dolly's trip had been too damned early; it had meant something other than that Leon was safely asleep and that she'd been going to Joe. He'd started his vigil at midnight and her brief stop in front of Joe's sleeping top had been only a few minutes after that. The freak show had closed at eleven-forty, not much over twenty minutes before then. Much too short a time for Leon to have had any drinks, undress and get to bed, be soundly enough asleep for Dolly to risk leaving him.

A thought came to him. What if Leon had gone to play poker in the gambling top? In that case Dolly might have taken the risk of a quick preliminary trip to Joe's to tell him about it. If that was the case everything would still work out—if only Leon didn't hit a winning streak that would keep him playing all night.

If that was it, had Joe got whatever Dolly had called out to him while she stood there? He didn't think so; if Joe had been inside and if Dolly had called, surely he'd have stuck his head out, not merely talked through canvas.

Too many ifs.

Another one had already struck him just about the time he'd started watching. What if Leon awakened when Dolly, maybe made over-confident by thinking his sleep was drugged, got up to leave him? Leon might beat and frighten the whole story out of her—and in that case might not Leon come knifing for him instead of or ahead of Joe Linder? That thought had sent him to the locked suitcase to get the gun he kept there, the snub-nosed .38 revolver. It was in his pocket now and its weight there was comforting when he thought of Leon and Leon's knives. At least he could get Leon before Leon could get him, whatever that might lead to. It wouldn't lead to anything except safety, of course, if Leon killed Dolly and Joe first. It would be even better that way except that he'd have to have a story for the cops as to why Leon would have chosen him as a third victim. Well, he as well as Joe could have been making passes at Dolly.

But damn it, was or wasn't Joe behind the enigmatic canvas of that sleeping top? If not, why not? He should surely, by now, be there waiting for Dolly.

Well, that much at least he could find out. No risk there and if Joe was home he could find out whether Dolly had called anything to him or whether she'd come but lost her nerve—and in that case what would he do now? The hell with deciding that now. Find out first if Joe was home.

He left the trailer and hurried over to the sleeping top. He called Joe's name and there wasn't any answer. Since at least he knew for sure that Dolly wasn't inside, he pulled back the flap and look in with his flashlight. No one.

He walked back to the trailer and sat on the steps, wondering if he should take the risk of going to the G-top.

But what if, while he was in there, Joe came back and Dolly joined him?

Someone was coming toward him in the darkness between two of the tops. Too late to get back into the trailer; whoever it was had seen him on the steps by now. He stood up and put his right hand into the pocket that held the gun, his hand clenching it ready to shoot. Then he saw who was coming and took his hand out of his pocket again. It was only Sammy.

"Hi, Mr. Evans," Sammy said. "Can I look at pitchers?"

"Not tonight, Sammy. You run right—Say, were you coming from the G-top?"

"Yeah, Mr. Evans. Jesse's playin' cards there."

"Who else is playing?"

"Uh, let's see, there's Jesse and Mr. King and Mr.—I forget his name, the man that throws knives, and, uh—"

"Joe Linder?"

"Yeah, Mr. Linder and—one or two more, but I can't remember, Mr. Evans."

"Thanks, Sammy. Now run along."

"Can't I please look at pitchers?"

"No."

"Gee, Mr. Evans, I won't bother you none. I'll just—" His hand lashed out and caught Sammy on the side of the face, a backhand blow. Not hard enough to hurt badly, but surprise made Sammy take a backward step and fall over a guy rope. He scrambled to his feet and ran toward the midway.

"Sammy, wait!" he called. When the kid kept on running, he swore to himself.

Why had he lost his temper and done a silly thing like that? Just because his nerves were tighter than piano strings and he hadn't thought. Now Sammy might go squawking to Jesse and—oh, hell, Jesse wouldn't make trouble over a little thing like that. Maybe tomorrow Jesse'd ask him why he'd hit the kid, and he'd have a good story for that, one that would put Sammy in the wrong. All he had to tell Jesse was about Sammy having come into his trailer while he wasn't there and getting into those pornography books. If he told Jesse that, Jesse would beat the hell out of Sammy.

And now that he remembered that, Sammy really had had that sock coming. Just the same, his hitting Sammy still worried him because it showed how tense he was inside. He'd better start calming down and controlling himself before he made a real mistake.

He strolled over to the G-top and went in. Sammy wasn't there, which was good; it meant he hadn't come running to Jesse. There was a nickel-and-dime crap game going on a blanket at one side, mostly rideboys and roustabouts. And six players at the poker table, Quintana and Linder among them. He strolled around behind Linder to watch.

On the pot that was being played everyone had thrown in their cards except Quintana and Barney King. Quintana had only a few dollars' worth of chips left in front of him but the pot was a big one There must have been a lot of raising and counter-raising if the game was still holding the usual dollar limit because the pot must have had well over twenty dollars in it. Barney said, "And one more to you," putting in two blue chips. Quintana picked up two blue chips to raise back and then hesitated and put in only one of them. "Call," he said. Barney said, "Four hooks," and put down his hand, four sevens. Quintana swore and threw in his cards. He counted his remaining chips and The Murderer counted them with him. One dollar one, two quarter ones and five dime ones, two bucks. The next hand he went into beyond the ante would break him unless he won with it.

The Murderer put his hand on the back of Linder's chair and let his forefinger tap Linder's shoulder blade twice. Then he strolled out. He heard Linder behind him say, "Deal me out one. Be right back."

He waited outside until Linder joined him and they walked far enough to be out of earshot. Then he said, "Dolly went to your place about half an hour ago. You weren't there so maybe she thinks you stood her up." Linder shook his head. "She knows what the score is now. She brought Quintana a sandwich, so she knows I'm playing in the game too. She knows I'll quit right after Leon does and be waiting after that."

"Good deal. Guess she went to your place before she knew that, to try to tell you Leon was playing and she might get there late or never."

"Not too late, it looks like now. Quintana had a run of luck for a while but it changed on him. Say, thanks again for fixing this up. If I can ever do anything—"

"Forget it, Joe. Dolly's a swell kid. She deserves a break and a chance to get away from that lousy bastard."

Linder's voice was a growl. "She'll get away all right."

Back in his trailer, The Murderer turned on the light and made himself a drink. Everything was on the beam again and he could even take a little time out before he went back to his watching. Even if Quintana had lost his remaining two bucks and was back in his quarters already, it would be a good half hour before Dolly would risk sneaking out on him.

The drink tasted good and helped his nerves a lot. He wouldn't pull another boner like hitting Sammy. Thinking about that reminded him, though, of something he'd been intending to do and had plenty of time for now. He took the pornography books from the compartment; it would be a good idea to keep them in a place where Sammy wouldn't be able to find them if he ever came back. He put them in one of the two compartments under the seats of the eating nook. Sammy would open doors and drawers but it would never occur to him to look for compartments that didn't show as such.

He finished his drink leisurely, then turned out the light and went back to the window.

Everything's going to be all right, he told himself; just keep calm, don't get excited or worried.

And gradually the panic came back to him, the realization that there were still a dozen ways in which his plan could go wrong.

Was it worth all this just to be able to finish the season and leave without anyone suspecting him? Why didn't he just run with the money, as he had planned to do if he hadn't been able to kill Mack Irby?

Why didn't he do it right now? The money, the gun, the disguise, the change of license plates for his car. People, including cops, would wonder why he'd disappeared, but would there be much of a search for him? Nobody knew about the money. He'd be safe unless Dolly blabbed and they started looking for him for killing Irby.

Wasn't every step he took increasing his risk instead of diminishing it?

He could be away from here in minutes. He made a point of keeping the car unhitched from the trailer and pointing outward so he could get it off the lot quickly.

Thirty seconds to grab the suitcase and take off in the car. Gun already in his pocket. And he knew, had already picked out, the alley off the main drag and just a few blocks from the lot where he could stop to change license plates and put on the quick disguise, the one that would serve until he'd have time to work out a permanent one.

Almost he decided to do it, this very instant.

But then he remembered that, no matter how well he did in building a new identity for himself, all the rest of his life would be hiding, fearing. And that if everything did go all right tonight, there'd be none of that. He'd be rich and safe beyond all question.

Again he was sweating.

CHAPTER SIXTEEN

Dolly heard footsteps and the scrape of lifting canvas, then Leon's voice. "Doll?"

For a second she held her intention to pretend that she was already asleep, then she realized that she wanted to know, had to know right this moment, whether he was back for the night or whether this was just an inspection trip. And also how late it was; the wait had seemed like many hours to her but that might have been because of her impatience. So she rolled over and said sleepily, "Yeah, Leon. Wha' time is it?"

"'Bout a quarter after one." That was good; it wasn't as late as she'd feared. She could see him now, sitting on his trunk and already twisting the cap off the whisky bottle. She saw him tilt it and heard the gurgle as he took a long drink. He put the bottle down. Then he was unbuttoning his shirt, pulling it out of his trousers. That meant he was staying. But it was cool; he'd hardly be taking off his shirt unless he intended to get right into bed and that might be the only drink he'd take. Would it be enough? Better get him talking. If she drank with him, he'd get started talking and keep on drinking while he talked.

She sat up. "Can I have a drink, Leon?" As he reached for the bottle to hand it to her she took the tumbler that was on her trunk and had it ready. "I'll pour a little in this. I'd rather just sip at it." She poured herself a short one in the tumbler, kept it in her hand as she gave him back the bottle. She'd just pretend to sip at it and when he wasn't looking, a little later, she'd pour it out on the ground. Or if she didn't get a chance to, she could probably drink it safely. Such a tiny drink, just one finger, wouldn't make her go to sleep if she fought against it. She asked, "How'd the poker go?"

Her hand around the tumbler concealed how little she'd poured. She tilted the glass back against closed lips and then lowered it, no longer bothering to conceal the quantity. He'd think she'd poured twice that much and had drunk half of it the first swallow.

Leon said, "Lousy." His voice was a growl but he wasn't really annoyed. He slid off the trunk without finishing taking off his shirt and sat on the ground instead, leaning back against the trunk. Making himself comfortable; it was all right now. He took another pull at the bottle.

He put the bottle down and opened his shirt to scratch his chest. Looking at him, Dolly wondered what had ever made her love him. He looked greasy. He wasn't, really; his skin was smooth to the touch, like a woman's, and he was proud of it, but maybe because it was so deep an olive color, it always looked as though it was oily even though it wasn't. And his hair so black and straight, always looked as though he'd plastered it down with vaseline.

No, he wasn't even handsome, although she'd thought him so once. His features were too regular, his eyes too darkly bright, staring at her so intently. Like a snake's eyes. And he moved sinuously and gracefully like a snake, like a boa constrictor, and with a boa's lazy strength, too.

His teeth flashed white in a sudden grin at her. "Anyway I got sense enough to know when to quit. Don't drop nearly a hundred bucks like some of those guys do sometimes. But damn, I wish my stake had lasted longer."

Dolly knew he didn't expect an answer.

He said, "Started off good. Then I got a flush and that son of a bitch King had a full. Half a dozen hands later I get a full myself, a aces full. And King's got four sevens."

He talked on. That was good; he felt like talking now and that meant he'd finish the bottle. And, in the process, get himself into a mellow mood which would be insurance against his wanting her when he finally came to bed.

"Y'know, Doll—you're a good kid. I don't always treat you right."

The sentimental vein already. Safe now. He never wanted her physically when he acted sentimental.

But she hurried to answer, "Sure you do, Leon," to reassure him because if she agreed that he treated her badly he'd turn sullen, then angry and—oh, it was so crazy the way he could like her and feel affection for her but could want her only when he was mad.

"Anyway, you're a good gal, Doll," he was saying. "And someday I'm going to hit a lucky streak an' buy you diamonds. Or maybe we'll have a show of our own and . . ." It, didn't matter what he said as long as he kept on drinking until the bottle was empty. And he did, and then he stood up and yawned. She poured out the rest of her whisky as he bent over the trunk to put down his shirt. He finished undressing down to the shorts he slept in and got under the blankets. "Night, Doll."

Within a minute his breathing was slow and regular. She thought, I'll count to a thousand slowly and if he hasn't moved or changed breathing—One-two-three— but other thoughts kept coming in. Somewhere in the eighties or nineties she lost track and started at eighty again just to be sure. But when she got a little past a hundred she lost track again and gave up, knowing she could never keep her mind on counting long enough to get to a thousand. Instead she let herself think for a while, for as long as she guessed to be about ten minutes, about what was going to happen so soon now.

Leon hadn't moved and his breathing hadn't changed except to get a little slower and a little louder, so she slid quietly out from under the covers. She hesitated, wondering whether to put on panties and bra, stockings. But that would be silly. She pulled off the slip and put the gingham dress on again, just that over her naked body. She stepped into slippers and went to the canvas sidewall. She stood there what must have been a full minute listening.

She raised the canvas only an inch at a time and only high enough for her to crawl under it, then stood listening again outside. Even through the canvas she could still hear his breathing, undisturbed.

She wanted to run now, but forced herself to walk quietly. Around behind the tops but not too far from them, keeping in the shadows as much as she could.

Then she stood in front of Joe's sleeping top. She looked around quickly to be sure nobody was watching. Evans' trailer, dark, stood near; if he was looking out the window he'd be seeing her, but that wouldn't matter; he already knew. And why, anyway, would he be watching? She hoped someday she'd be able to pay him back for what he'd done for her tonight.

No one was in sight and she went in quickly without calling out. Joe's arms were around her almost before the flap fell. He whispered, "Dolly!" Then he was kissing her.

CHAPTER SEVENTEEN

The murderer sighed with relief. Dolly had got away from Leon and now she was with Joe. The first hurdle.

He'd glanced at his watch just as she'd gone in. Six minutes after two o'clock. Give them till half past, he decided. Twenty-four minutes, just to be sure, in case they did any talking first. Not that it really mattered how Quintana found them; he'd kill them just for being alone together. But hell, why not be kind to Joe and Dolly and let them have a little time together, as long as it wasn't long enough that there'd be any chance of Dolly leaving to go back to her own bed? Give them that much of a break, at least. Twenty-four minutes. Maybe thirty overall, counting the time it would take him to start the ball rolling.

He checked himself while he waited. He had the razor blade. The gun he hoped he wouldn't have to use—and wouldn't have to unless a wheel came off somewhere. He was wearing the crepe soled shoes that let him walk silently. If things went wrong, the car was ready.

And now it was half past two.

He left the trailer and went quietly around behind the tops until he found the freak show top, the corner of it where Quintana would be sleeping. He looked around carefully to be sure no one was in sight and then took out the razor blade, a Gem blade that had only one edge and a stiff back, and made a six-inch slit in the canvas. He held the slit open a little and put his eye to it. He could see perfectly; there was more light in there than here outside. The bedding. Quintana asleep on it, lying on his back. He could even hear Quintana's breathing.

He made his voice sepulchral. "Leon Quintana!"

No movement. He said it again, just a trifle louder. He saw Quintana's head raise.

Quickly now, before he got thoroughly awake. "Your wife is with Joe Linder, in Joe's top."

Quintana was sitting up fast now, so he got away from there quickly and silently, back to his own trailer.

Again he stood in the dark watching through the window. Almost at once Quintana came in sight running. He wore only a pair of shorts but he had two knives, one in each hand—and held not for throwing but as a knife fighter holds them. He shouldered his way through the flap and there was a scream.

He shuddered.

Almost instantly carneys were coming running from several directions, mostly from the freak show top where a lot of them slept on or under the bally platforms. Dixie, the sword swallower, and Frank the magician were the first ones out in the open. And then Admiral Tim, the midget, came running after them on his tiny legs, looking, in his underwear, more like a child than ever.

They were standing, looking around, the three of them, still trying to guess where that horrible scream had come from, when Quintana came out of the sleeping top. There was blood on him, and he still held a knife in either hand and both of the knives were dripping.

He looked at Dixie and the Admiral and Frank and then dropped both knives and sat down on the ground, put both bloody hands over his face and started to sob.

Others were coming up now. A knot of people was forming around the sleeping top and somebody with a flashlight went inside but came out quickly. Nobody touched Quintana but Dixie carefully kicked first one and then the other of the knives away, out of Quintana's reach.

Smitty, the bookkeeper, came up in a bathrobe, asked a few questions and then took off on the run. He'd be going to phone for the police or an ambulance or both.

And now was the time to find out, to be sure. There were enough people around that it was all right for him to go there too. And he was still set for his getaway if he learned that either Dolly or Joe was alive.

He left the trailer and went over to the knot of people around the sleeping top. He touched Barney King's shoulder. "What happened, Barney?"

"Dolly was in there with Linder. Quintana killed them."

"God. Killed both of them?"

Barney nodded.

Still, he wanted to be sure, to be completely sure. He pushed his way past the others to the flap, pushed it aside and looked in with his flashlight.

Quietly he backed away.

He wouldn't have to make a getaway. Not tonight, not ever. He was safe now.

He stayed with the crowd a while; it was a crowd by now, hung around with it until the sound of approaching police sirens started to melt the crowd away. He went back to his trailer then, undressed in the dark and got into bed.

Safe, completely safe. Everything had worked perfectly.

But he wished he'd taken Barney's word that they were both dead instead of looking inside. He knew it would be a long time before he'd forget what he'd seen there.

It was a long time before he could get to sleep and twice he wakened from dreams that weren't exactly nightmares but still weren't nice things to be dreaming.

CHAPTER EIGHTEEN

It had been daylight for several hours before the light in Dr. Magus's eyes brought him near enough the threshold of consciousness to make him turn over and bury his face in the pillow. But the act of turning brought him across that threshold, unreturnably across. Moving his head had done it; movement had wakened the little monsters inside his skull and they had immediately picked up their pneumatic drills and started trying to drill their way out through his forehead and temples. Others with pickaxes and peaveys started chipping away at the backs of his eyeballs. And simultaneously he became aware of the taste in his mouth; it was a taste which he knew well and which experience had taught him could be removed only by quantities of ice water.

He groaned and sat up, moving slowly and carefully.

Yesterday's hangover was as nothing to this one. This was one that only heroic treatment could help.

He pulled on trousers and a shirt, the first of each that came to hand, then got cautiously to his feet and stepped into a pair of old slippers.

A bucket and a two-quart tin pail. With one in either hand he went out onto the midway and trudged toward the chow top. Few carneys seemed to be up and about although the length of Dr. Magus's shadow ahead of him told him that it must be almost nine o'clock. His shadow carried a bucket and a pail too; he felt sorry for it if it felt as bad as he did.

In the chow top he put pail and bucket on the counter and sank down onto a stool in front of it. "Fill 'em, huh, Hank?"

"Sure, Doc. First time you've brought them in a month. Same like last time?"

"Yes, Hank. And please hurry. I am dying."

He watched while Hank went to the soft drink cooler and picked out a chunk of ice as big as his head. Hank put it in the bucket and then held the bucket under the water tap until it was about half full. From the coffee urn he filled the smaller pail with steaming black java. "Let's see, Doc, it's no cream, no sugar, ain't it?"

"Right," Dr. Magus said.

He carried the pail and bucket back to the mitt camp without having tasted either. The coffee would still be too hot and the water wouldn't be really cold yet. He put both of them on the ground and sat beside them and next to the foot locker, from which he took two mugs and a big bandana handkerchief. He dipped one mug into the ice water and drank deeply, sighed deeply as the outer layer of the horrible taste washed away. He filled it and drank once more. Then he dipped the bandana in the bucket and tied it around his head without wringing it out. Cold water ran down his face and neck but he didn't bother to wipe it off. He dipped the other mug into the coffee pail, dipping only a small quantity so it wouldn't be too hot to drink. He sipped it and decided he'd live. The next step would be a cup of coffee laced with whisky.

A voice from outside called, "Hey, Doc, you home?"

"I'm beginning to think so. Come on in."

It was Showalter, the lieutenant. He stood just inside and looked down at Dr. Magus. He said, "Brother. Do you feel as bad as you look?"

"Fortunately, Lieutenant, I do not know how I look so I cannot make the comparison. And please do not tell me how I look; it is a matter which at the moment arouses no interest in me. Please sit down so I can see you without bending my head so far back."

He finished the coffee in the mug and dipped the other mug into the ice water again; it was quite cold by now. He drank half of the contents and poured the other half over the bandana handkerchief on his head.

"And now," he said. "will you be so kind as to hand me that whisky bottle? Helping yourself to a drink if you wish."

The lieutenant didn't take a drink but his eyes widened a bit as he saw the label on the bottle. "Old Bushmills. That stuff costs money, Doc. You always drink it?"

"I do not. Special celebration last night. My fifty-third birthday. Or I think it was. Today's my hundredth." He dipped the coffee mug into the pail again and added whisky from the bottle. He sipped. "Lieutenant, if you share the general delusion that expensive whisky leaves one with less of a hangover than does cheap whisky, disabuse yourself of the idea at once. It is quite the other way around, in fact. With good whisky the hangover is worse because its taste is so smooth that one inevitably drinks much more than one would of lesser liquor."

"This place smells like you took a bath in it. Say, Doc, were you a witness last night?"

"Not that I know of. A witness to what?"

"A witness to the murders." Showalter's eyes were on Dr. Magus's face. "Good God, you mean you slept through the slaughter last night and still don't know about it?"

"I do. What happened?"

"Dolly Quintana and Joe Linder. Quintana killed both of them, caught 'em in the act, in Linder's tent."

Dr. Magus swore luridly and at length.

"Doc, what time did you go to sleep?"

"I don't—it couldn't have been much after midnight."

"But you must've been out this morning to get that coffee and the ice. You didn't talk to anybody at all?"

"Only to the counterman in the chow top, Lieutenant. I guess Hank must have assumed that I already knew about it, though, or he would certainly have told me."

"I should think he'd have said something about it even if he thought you knew."

"He saw I was in no mood for conversation, I presume. When did it happen?"

"We got the call at two-forty a.m. It happened only minutes before that."

"Have you got Quintana? Or did he run?"

"Didn't even try to run. And we've got his confession, signed and in detail. Not that we'd need it. He was sitting there on the ground in front of the tent, crying, blood all over him and the knives, two of them, right near. But just the same—Doc, the other carneys pretty much know you and like you, don't they?"

"In general, I believe so. Why?"

"Look, maybe you can do me a favor. We want to find some witnesses to this thing last night. One or more people who actually saw Quintana coming out of the tent with the knives still in his hands. And the first arrivals did see him—that's the story we get only it's always second hand. Everybody we talk to knows there were some others who got there first, only they don't know who or won't tell us. We want to find some who actually saw Quintana before he dropped the knives."

"But why, if you have a signed confession from him?"

"There's always a chance a guy will repudiate a confession, change his mind and claim we beat him into signing it or something, see? In this case, we can pin it on him anyway. I'm pretty sure. But it'll be easier, more positive, if we've got those first witnesses lined up, just in case."

"I see. But where do I come in? I wasn't one of them."

"Because you can find out who they are. The carneys won't give you the same runaround they give us."

"Possibly. But if they have not—ah, what is the phrase?—come forward, then it's because they don't want to. And for obvious reasons. They would hate to be subpoenaed to come back here for the trial from possibly thousands of miles away. You can't blame them, Lieutenant."

"Yeah, that I understand. But, Doc, if you find out who they are I don't ask you to give me their names. You wouldn't do that even if I asked. But I'd like you to talk to them like a Dutch uncle, explain to them that there's only the slimmest chance we'll ever need them, but if that chance comes up, they wouldn't want Quintana to go free on this, would they? You carneys stick together, yeah, but not when it's a deal like last night. None of them would be on Quintana's side, would they?"

"None of them, I'm sure. As little sympathy as carneys have with the Law, there is a limit to what they will condone in one another. Besides, Dolly and Joe were carneys too, and both of them much better liked than Quintana."

"That's what I figured, Doc. And you personally, you wouldn't want to see Quintana beat the chair, would you?"

"I personally—" Dr. Magus stopped to refill his coffee mug, two-thirds from the coffee pall and the rest finishing off what was left in the whisky bottle. And to let himself think. He personally thought Quintana was a psychopath, a person who needed to be shut away by society for its own protection, but to be pitied rather than hated, a person who, though not insane by legal definition, would more justly be placed in an asylum for the criminally insane than in the electric chair. But why argue the point? He said, "I personally would be glad to throw the switch, if your sovereign state requires such assistance."

"Attaboy, Doc. Then find out who those witnesses were and talk to them, huh? Talk them into coming to us and letting us get signed statements from them—and it's a thousand to one we'll ever need more than that. And listen—was Mack Irby well liked?"

"Fairly well. Why?"

"Another argument for you. Quintana killed Irby."

Dr. Magus's eyebrows raised. "He confessed that too?"

"Nope, won't admit it. But we found Irby's dough— two hundred and forty bucks, just about what we predicted. It was rolled up and stuffed in the bell of a cornet in Quintana's trunk."

"Couldn't that be coincidence? I mean, couldn't it have been Quintana's own money hidden there, just happening to be about the right amount?"

"Nope, Doc. I'll tell you how we're positive. We didn't give this out before because we didn't want the murderer to know it, but I can tell you now. I made a trip to Glenrock, to the bank where he cashed that two-grand check and bought traveler's checks with eighteen hundred of it. And since it was only the day before and the amount had been pretty big—big enough so they telephoned the insurance company to make sure the check was okay—the teller remembered the deal. And he remembered he'd asked Irby how he'd wanted the two hundred cash and Irby said ten twenties would be okay. And the teller counted the ten twenties off a stack of new ones that had just come in, fresh off the press and with consecutive serial numbers, see? He couldn't tell us the exact serial numbers because they used others of them too, but they knew the series and approximately how the numbers would run."

"And those twenties were in Quintana's trunk?"

"All ten of them. Brand new, serial numbers consecutive and just about the serial numbers the teller said they'd be. The other forty bucks was in old bills, tens and fives; that's the money Irby had with him at the time of the accident less whatever he spent in the hospital."

"I'll be damned," Dr. Magus said.

And he meant it. He'd always figured Quintana, because of his psychopathic jealousy, as an accident going somewhere to happen. But he'd never figured him as a killer for money. Even now, he couldn't see Quintana in that role. If Quintana had killed Irby it seemed more likely that he suspected Irby of making a pass at Dolly and had killed him for that reason, taking the money to make it look like a robbery kill. Although two hundred forty bucks is worth taking along if it's in your victim's pocket, even though it isn't the reason why you killed him.

But if Quintana's motive had been jealousy, it would have to be from something that had happened more than seven weeks before the murder, some slight thing Quintana had brooded over and built bigger during Irby's absence. Certainly he hadn't had time to make a pass at Dolly Monday night.

Apparently Showalter had been thinking along the same lines, although with less information. He said thoughtfully, "It's funny, Doc. Anybody but Quintana, I'd figure it was Dolly who was with Irby Monday night. With Quintana's knowledge, to finger him for the robbery. The old game. But damn it, he was too crazy jealous of her for it to have been that. What's your guess, Doc? Could it have been Dolly with Irby and Quintana not jealous about it because he'd put her up to it?"

"Ummm," Dr. Magus said. He knew damned well Dolly hadn't been with Irby because it had been Maybelle. But that still wasn't any of the lieutenant's business. He said, "I don't think so. But how's this for a possibility? Leon wakes up and finds Dolly gone. To the doniker, as he learns later, but he doesn't know that. Goes out hunting for her. Tries Jesse's top because he knows how often it's used for assignations. Hadn't brought a knife so picks up a tent stake. Makes noise coming and Irby crawls out—or maybe was crawling out just then anyway for another purpose—and he kills Irby before bothering to make sure it's Dolly he's been with. Goes on in to kill Dolly—but it isn't Dolly."

Showalter looked doubtful. "I suppose it could have happened that way, but wouldn't the woman have told us? If she'd known Quintana killed the guy she was sleeping with would she still have kept her mouth shut?"

"Couple of possibilities. Scared of Quintana and thought it would be her word against his. Or more likely, she's somebody's wife—not Quintana's, but he's not the only jealous guy in the world—and couldn't give Quintana away without admitting she'd shacked up with Irby."

"I won't buy it. I think Quintana would have killed her too, to be sure she didn't talk. Nope, I think it must after all have been a straight robbery kill."

Dr. Magus said, "I wonder why Quintana hasn't confessed to it, though. Three murders can't get him in worse trouble than two."

"The hell they can't. And that's another thing makes me think the Irby kill was for money. On the double murder it's just possible that a good mouthpiece might get him life instead of the chair, claiming heat of passion and non-premeditation. But if the Irby deal was a cold, planned kill for money and he confessed to it, he'd get the chair for sure."

The lieutenant lighted a cigarette and drew on it thoughtfully. "Besides, confessing to it wouldn't fit in with the insanity plea I figure he's going to make."

"What makes you think that?"

"Well, for one thing he acts like he's trying to act crazy. For another, his story of how he found out Dolly was with Joe Linder. Says he heard a voice in his sleep telling him so."

"How do you suppose he did find out, Lieutenant?"

"Same like you suggested on the Irby deal, woke up and found her gone. And probably had some reason to suspect Joe Linder so he went looking in the right place."

He lighted a cigarette and took a deep drag. "Well, anyway, Doc, the carneys can quit panicking."

"Panicking? I hadn't seen any."

"Maybe I didn't mean it that strong. But plenty of them have been scared ever since the Irby kill. I been damn near living on the lot, and I could feel it. And listen, the postal savings window at the p.o. downtown has been doing a land office business since Monday. While there was a guy on the lot who'd kill for money, nobody wanted heavy sugar around. Some of the boys and gals here put in amounts that kind of surprised me."

"Most of us try to get enough ahead so we won't have to work during the winter, Lieutenant. I suppose you were in close touch with the p.o. because they were watching for those new twenties with consecutive serials."

"Yeah. Well, it's washed up now, Doc. Hope, though, that we can get Quintana to make it a really clean washup by confessing to the Irby kill."

He stood up. "Well, we'll fry him on one count if not the other. And you'll try to find those witnesses and try to talk them into talking to me?"

"I'll try, Lieutenant. At least I'll keep my ears open. But I can't guarantee any results."

"Okay, I understand that. Thanks."

He left.

The rest of the coffee was cold but Dr. Magus decided he felt well enough to tackle the next step in recovery, a big hot breakfast. The thought of eating one was terrible but it was the only thing that would make him feel human before evening short of starting in to drink again, and that would only postpone the evil day. He took off the soaking bandana and his shirt, which was almost as wet. He found a towel and dried himself, combed his hair and beard and put on a clean shirt. It was easier to make the chow top this time. One more cup of hot coffee and then breakfast. Eating it was a fight, but he won.

Nothing worse than a dull headache as he walked back to the mitt camp, and that would go away soon.

Ten by ten feet square, the mitt camp. He paced one side of it, three paces one way and three paces back. Last night he'd had a brilliant idea in connection with finding the money. But what had the idea been?

He remembered a flash in the crystal. Unless it had been something in his own head, back of his eyeballs. It had been while he'd been concentrating on where the money might be hidden. He'd thought of the generator car and had decided it couldn't mean that. Nor a fuse box.

And he remembered trying to calculate how big a package forty-two grand would make and had decided on a minimum size, the size of a cigar box. Could be bigger of course, but he wouldn't have to worry about looking in smaller repositories. Two hundred forty dollars you could stuff into a cornet, but not forty-two thousand. Not unless it was in the form of forty-two thousand-dollar bills and it wouldn't be.

What in—Suddenly he remembered. He'd decided to go to Glenrock to see if he could get a lead at the hospital there.

For a moment he thought disgustedly, hell, if that's all the idea was—

But then its possibilities began to come to him. With a good enough song and dance to use at the hospital, he might get a lead to the money even if it wasn't hidden with the carnival. He might find out whom Irby had communicated with while he was in the hospital. He might get a break by learning that Irby had been worried about a suitcase that had been checked somewhere and had sent a check or money order to cover storage charges so it would be held for him. He might have made a long distance phone call or sent a telegram.

It would take slick con work, a really good song and dance, to get details like that from people as professionally reticent as doctors and nurses, but it might be done.

It was worth trying.

He dug a railroad map out of his foot locker to check on how difficult it might be to get there. It wasn't difficult at all. Both Bloomfield and Glenrock were on the main trunk line of the B. & O. There ought to be several trains a day between them and the trip would be just long enough to let him get completely past his hangover.

Another day lost from work, more money spent, but what did that matter compared to a chance at a beautiful hunk of moolah like forty-two grand?

• • •

There is a tide in the affairs of men, which, taken at the flood, leads on to fortune; omitted, all the voyage of their life is bound in shallows and in miseries.

Anyway, that was what Brutus had said. And Cassius answer? Then, with your will, go on.

Cassius, I am on my way.

Half an hour later, as dapper and at least outwardly as cheerful as he'd been yesterday, he ran into Lieutenant Showalter near the entrance gate.

Showalter grinned at him. "Doc, you sure look better than you did when I first saw you this morning. I wasn't sure you were going to live."

"Nor was I, Lieutenant."

He started on past but the lieutenant said, "Just a second, Doc. I just got some news. You can forget what I asked you to do about finding those witnesses."

"Oh?" Dr. Magus asked. He had already forgotten it. He had had no faint intention of ever trying.

"Quintana ain't going to change his mind about that confession. Just got word, he killed himself in his cell. The guy had guts, or else he really was crazy. Want to know what the son of a bitch did?"

Dr. Magus had a hunch that he didn't want to know.

"We thought we'd taken away anything he could use to kill himself with—but we didn't think to knock his teeth out. He bit open the vein in one of his wrists. And d'ya want to know what he did while he was bleeding to death?"

"No," said Dr. Magus firmly. "Please forgive me but I do not want to know."

He walked on rapidly, feeling a little sick.

CHAPTER NINETEEN

The murderer felt lousy. Nervous, jittery, keyed-up.

And worried that he should feel that way for no reason at all. All of his problems were solved. He was safe.

Everything had worked out better than he'd dared hope. The cops had even written off Mack Irby's murder. Now even if they got him for stealing the money—and he didn't see how they could ever do that anyway with the bills not marked or in consecutive numbers—they'd never suspect him of having murdered to get it. Why, he hadn't even stolen it; he'd found it accidentally and what was illegal about that? Of course if they could prove it was stolen property they could take it away from him, but how could they do more than that?

The way in which he'd got rid of the only witness against him, Dolly, had been a master stroke. A perfect crime, because he hadn't done it himself; he'd pulled strings like a puppeteer and Dolly and Joe and Leon had danced to his pulling. Why had he been worried that anything could go wrong? Last night for a few minutes he'd almost been panicky enough to run away before waiting to see how it worked out.

Hadn't had enough confidence in himself, that's all.

Oh, there'd been luck on his side too. Quintana's killing himself in jail this morning, for instance. But that just made things a little better; it hadn't been necessary. They had Quintana figured for Mack Irby's murder anyway—what a brilliant thought it had been to give that money to Dolly!—but now he couldn't keep on denying he'd killed Irby until maybe they began to doubt, however slightly, that he had.

And it had been lucky Quintana had told them he'd heard "a voice in his sleep" telling him Dolly was with Joe. Not important but a nice touch.

There wasn't a way on earth they could touch him now for murder. And there wasn't anybody besides himself who even suspected Charlie and Mack had robbed a bank.

Everything was perfect. Charlie and Mack dead. Dolly, Joe, Quintana dead.

Then why was he feeling lousy today?

Conscience? Hell, he didn't have any conscience. That was a lot of crap. It hadn't bothered him in the slightest to kill Mack Irby—except of course when he walked out onto the midway with the stake in his hand and Dolly had seen it. Dolly? Just because she was a dame? Nuts. Anyway, he hadn't killed her; Quintana had. And for big money you couldn't be squeamish.

He'd killed twice before in his life and neither time had it bothered him for five minutes. Of course both of those times had been back when, during the depression, he'd been on the bum or on the grift. The time on the freight train when he'd red-lighted the loud-mouthed shade. The time when he'd mugged the lush in the alley back of Clark Street in Chicago. Yes, he had to admit neither of those had been premeditated murders. He'd pushed the brakeman off the moving train in sudden anger, the same blind anger that had made him strike Sammy last night. And he hadn't really meant to kill the lush he rolled, just to make him unconscious would have been enough. But they were murders just the same. They'd have fried him for either one.

What he needed, he thought, was a good drunk. A two-weeks knockdown-dragout drunk. But that would have to wait until after the end of the season.

There was a knock on the trailer door. He said, "Come in," and then, "Hi, Wiggins. Sit down. Too early for a drink? I was just thinking about one."

"Too early for me. Can't stay anyway. I'm just passing word around the lot about the funerals. Dolly's and Linder's. Both tomorrow morning at an undertaker's downtown, Gresham's. We didn't figure under the circumstances it could be a double funeral but we're having them one right after the other. Dolly's at ten, Linder's at eleven. Think you can make 'em?"

"I'll try."

"Good. We'd like a good turnout. Make it if you can."

Wiggins turned to leave. The Murderer said, "Hey, wait a minute. You going to be downtown today, Wiggy?"

"Sure. Be leaving here within half an hour."

"Wonder if you'll do something for me. I won't be leaving the lot today at all and tomorrow morning would be kind of late. Will you have a florist send some flowers for both funerals?"

"Be glad to. And I've got to go to a florist's anyway."

The Murderer took a twenty out of his wallet, then hesitated and took out another.

"Make it twenty for each."

Wiggins took the money. "Any special kind of flowers?"

"I wouldn't know one kind from another anyway. Flowers are flowers. Say, I hear Quintana killed himself. Not going to be a funeral for him, is there?"

"That son of a bitch? Let the state bury him—or stuff him in a garbage can. You want anything special on either card to go with the flowers?"

"Just my name." He hesitated and then said, "Yeah, just my name."

"Okay. Be seeing you."

After Wiggins left, he lifted a dinette seat and took out the whisky bottle. He'd allow himself one drink, one only. Then no more till after closing time late this evening; he'd allow himself two or three then.

Just one drink now to drive away the jitters. He'd damned near done a foolish thing just now; he'd damned near told Wiggins to put the word, "Sorry," on the card with Dolly's flowers. That would have been foolish, all right. Not because it would have made anyone suspect anything; he was safely past any danger of that. But it would have been foolish because he'd have been admitting to himself that he was sorry. Getting sentimental and silly. That could be dangerous if he let it get him. And anyway Dolly couldn't read the card so it wouldn't mean anything.

He put back the whisky bottle and noticed alongside it the pile of pornography books he'd moved there last night from the compartment where Sammy had found them. He picked up the top one and started to kill a bit of time looking through it.

And, realizing something, he started to grin.

That's what was wrong with him! He hadn't had a woman for over six weeks now, since he'd found the money! Hadn't even thought about it!

He'd been so busy making plans so he could keep that money, so busy looking forward to the hedonistic future it would give him, that he'd forgotten the present.

What reason was there why he couldn't have a woman tonight?

Not that he wanted a permanent tie-up with any of these cheap carney broads. He had better plans than that, but those plans couldn't start for a couple of weeks.

No, even after he could start spending money freely he didn't want any tie-ups. Cheaper and in the long run better to pay for it. Like many hedonistic and highly sexed men, he basically disliked women. He liked to use their bodies but had only contempt for them otherwise. Sleep with one, yes. Live with one, never. So much simpler when one could afford it, as he'd been able to do although not as often as he liked for several years now, just to pay a woman for the use of her body than to go through the boring motions of being nice to one so you could talk her into bed for free. And, if he wanted a rematch, having to try to please her as well as himself; that took two-thirds of the pleasure away. Above all, he hated sentiment, hated to pretend to feel it when he didn't, hated too the very thought that a woman might ever feel sentimental toward him. Sentiment was a lot of crap and the only way to avoid even the pretense of it was to pay for what you got, right down the line.

Naturally, he thought of Trixie Connor.

There were several girls on the lot who'd put out for cash, most of them strictly among the other carneys. For most of the season he'd had one or another of them in his trailer two or three times a week. Always Trixie when he'd been feeling flush; she was the most expensive thing on the lot but worth the difference if you could afford it. There were pigs like the waitress in the grab joint who'd spend the night with you for a fin; Trixie wanted that for a quick flop and twenty to spend the night, so he hadn't had Trixie too often— mostly because he wanted all night or nothing and twenty bucks several times a week ran into heavy money.

But hell, now he could afford to have Trixie all night and every night for the rest of the season if he wanted to. Well, he couldn't go that far; he didn't want to start acting suddenly prosperous, even now. But it wouldn't be out of character for him to have Trixie come to the trailer tonight and a few more nights before the season was over. In fact he'd been acting out of character not to have had her or any other woman there for six weeks or so.

Naturally he was jittery and nervous.

He put the book back and looked at his watch. A good time to make the date; she'd be getting ready for the model show to open. Time for him to leave the trailer anyway and get with his own show.

He strolled over to the model show top. He went back inside and called out Trixie's name; she came under the canvas partition that shut off the dressing space. "Hi," she said. "Haven't seen you for a long time."

"Hi yourself, Trixie. Just decided it's been too damn long a time." He dropped his voice. "Busy tonight?"

"Well, I promised someone I'd see him right after we close, but it's not an all-night date."

"Good. Want to drop around to my trailer after that?"

"Sure," she said. "Be there by one at the latest."

CHAPTER TWENTY

The hospital waiting-room was paneled in knotty pine and the sofa and two chairs were covered with cool green leather. The pictures on the walls were reproductions of a Rembrandt and an Utrillo.

Behind a massive mahogany desk, only the receptionist struck a discordant note; she was a faded blonde placidly chewing gum and shuffling cards from an index file.

Dr. Magus waited patiently until she looked up. He said, "I beg your pardon. I would like, if possible, to talk to the doctor who treated my son here about two months ago. I am Dr. Ranee Irby. My son's name was

John MacGregor Irby, but I understand that he gave his name here as Mack Irby."

"Whatsa doctor's name?"

"I'm afraid I'll have to ask you that, my dear. It should show on your records. The name is Irby, I-r-b-y."

She reached for the index file and then hesitated. "Irby—wasn't he one of the two carneys brought here after a accident, talker for a unborn show?"

She'd been a carney herself, Dr. Magus knew now. That made her a human being, but he couldn't risk showing it. He said carefully, "He worked for a carnival. In what capacity, I do not know. I had not seen him for many years."

"I remember him. He had a broken leg. The other fella was killed."

"That's right."

"Dr. Kramer took care of him, then. He was resident here and he'd of been the only doctor around at night. It was at night they brought him here."

"You say Dr. Kramer was the resident physician? You mean that he is no longer with you?"

"Yeah. He's in Cincinnati now. On the staff at Miseracordia Hospital there."

Dr. Magus sighed. "Unfortunate. But perhaps I might talk to whichever nurse would remember him best?"

"Well—I guess so. Only I wouldn't know which one. You better talk to Miss Plackett, the head nurse."

"Is Miss Plackett here now?"

"She ain't on duty but she's probally in her room. Sid-down and wait. I'll ring for her."

Dr. Magus sat down and waited, musing on the sad fate of a carney forced to work as receptionist in a hospital and on the sad fate of a hospital so short of help that it was forced to hire a receptionist who used such atrocious grammar. He didn't know which was the worse.

A tall woman with graying hair came into the reception room. Years of experience enabled Dr. Magus to size her up at a quick glance. Sharp eyes, sharp nose. Sharp manner too, no doubt, and tough to work for, but soft as butter down inside. Easy to handle. She wasn't in uniform; she wore a severely cut navy blue suit.

The blonde said, "This gemmun wants to talk to you, Miss Plackett."

Dr. Magus rose, bowed slightly and smiled. His number one smile. "Miss Plackett, I am Dr. Ranee Irby. My son, I understand, spent almost seven weeks here, up to last Monday afternoon, with a broken leg and other but minor injuries. Which of your nurses would be most familiar with the case?"

"I believe I myself would, Dr. Irby. I helped Dr. Kramer the night Mr. Irby was brought in, and I am familiar with the progress of the case up to the time he was released. Just what is it you wish to know?"

Dr. Magus sighed. "Many little things, Miss Plackett. Not the medical details nor anything that could be considered confidential. Perhaps—Do you know my son is dead?"

"I know the police came here a few days ago and asked questions about him. They didn't tell us why."

"Because he was killed only hours after he left here. I am told that he returned immediately to the carnival he worked for and met his death there that same night."

"I am sorry to hear that, doctor." She wasn't, really. But she would be after he got into the song and dance Dr. Magus hadn't started yet. But it was about time he did.

He said, "Thank you. I—Miss Plackett, I'm sure you'll be able to help me better if I explain fully to you just what my interest is—and it's really a bit complex, almost impossible to tell you briefly. Nor would I blame you for not wanting to answer my questions until I have explained. I wonder—Will you forgive me if I ask you to have dinner with me? It will give us time to talk."

"Why, I—"

"I'll appreciate it greatly, Miss Plackett. And there is so much to tell you before I even know what questions I want to ask."

"Well, I believe I can, doctor. Thank you."

He waited while she got hat and handbag, then asked her to choose where they should go, since he was a stranger in town. There was a nice restaurant, she said, only a block from the hospital. They walked there.

He was pleasantly surprised to be able to talk her into a cocktail before dinner.

"I should perhaps explain, Miss Plackett, that I am not a doctor of medicine. My doctorate is in philosophy. I am a professor of psychology at U. S. C.—University of Southern California." He smiled. "Psychology is a field which, in all modesty, I can say I know thoroughly—with one reservation. For whatever reason, I failed with John."

"John?"

"My son. I understand he is on your records as Mack Irby; his full name is, or was, John MacGregor Irby. He ran away from home at the age of eighteen, eleven years ago. Just two months after he completed high school. I have not seen him since, nor heard of or from him until yesterday when I was told of his death, and what is known of the circumstances surrounding it, by the Los Angeles Police Department."

"But how did they know? I mean, if he'd changed his name and—"

"Through his fingerprints, taken as a matter of police routine after his death. They were sent to Washington and found to be those of my son which were on record because he'd been arrested several times during the last year he was still living at home.

"So the Los Angeles police were notified and notified me. They didn't have many details but I telephoned the carnival they said he'd been with and talked with a Mr.

Wiggins there—he seemed to be one of the partners who own the carnival—and learned all I could learn from him, which included the fact that John had just returned to the carnival after having spent seven weeks here. I made immediate arrangements to fly East to learn more about the matter. Since Glenrock is west of Bloomfield, I decided to stop here first to see what I could learn at the hospital before I continue on to the carnival."

"I—see. But there's nothing—"

"Miss Plackett, my son was murdered. But I am not investigating his murder. The murderer has already been apprehended. He was another employee of the carnival, a knife thrower. He was arrested for another crime but my son's money, definitely identified, was found concealed in his trunk. That money was the motive and there is no mystery in connection with my son's death."

"But then what—I don't understand, Dr. Irby."

"The mystery of my son's life. Until he was fourteen years old, John was a normal, happy, healthy boy. Something happened then—or possibly a delayed reaction to something that happened sooner—that changed him. He began to rebel against authority—mine, the school's, the state's. He began to steal and to—to do other things. I tried my honest best to find out what had happened to him. I tried to talk to him but he was sullen and uncommunicative; he grew farther and farther away from me. And at eighteen he ran away from home.

"I tried to trace him every way I could. But the news I got yesterday—the news that he is dead—was the first word in eleven years. And now—but I suppose you see what I'm getting at, Miss Plackett?"

"Why—not exactly."

"I want to know where I made my mistake in dealing with my son, what happened to him inside, what kind of a man he became and why. You see, I've got to know. Aside from parental love, there is the fact that I am supposed to be a psychologist. God help me, the university has been wanting me to conduct a seminar in child guidance. How can I, and not feel dishonest, when I still do not know where I went wrong in guiding my own son?

"For the sake of my professional pride as well as for the sake of my own conscience and my integrity as a teacher of others, I must find the answer."

Dr. Magus took a deep breath. He was hitting his stride now, beginning to feel the role. And he had his audience with him; Miss Plackett's nose was still sharp but her eyes weren't. They looked at him understanding, compassionately. She asked, "But how can I help you, doctor? We didn't get to know him well, certainly not well enough to hazard a guess as to—to what you want to find out about."

Dr. Magus didn't answer directly. He said, "How long it takes me doesn't matter. I am due for a sabbatical year. I had planned to take it year after next, but I shall make arrangements to make it this coming term, if necessary. I am going to find and talk to every friend he had, every woman he knew. I am going to trace back and back to every place he lived or worked, until I find the answer. Somewhere along the line he must have talked to someone about his early life, must have said something which—combined with what I already know—will give me the key to that hidden room in his mind.

"He had a good home, Miss Plackett. He was an only child. We were far from wealthy but he had everything he needed, as much as the boys he went to school with had; there was no reason for him to feel inferior to or jealous of his contemporaries. I was not too severe with him, I am sure, nor do I believe we spoiled or pampered him. His mother was an angel—" Dr. Magus stared off into space. His eyes watered.

"Was?" asked Miss Packett softly.

"Yes, she died five years ago. And he loved his mother. I know that. Yet after he left home eleven years ago he never wrote her once, not so much as a postcard. She died not knowing what had happened to him.

"Yet he loved her. Can you not see how puzzling that fact alone is, how strongly indicative that there was something, some factor which I hope is not beyond my understanding, which I can learn about and, having learned, understand my own son?"

"I—I understand, doctor, fully. I don't know how I can help you, but I'll gladly try."

"Thank you. And I believe you understand now why I came here first—not only because geographically it was on my way to the carnival, but because except for the last few hours my son spent the last seven weeks of his life in your care. And what do I want to know about those seven weeks?" He gestured helplessly. "I don't know, specifically. So I want to know everything you can tell me. I want to know what my son was like, after eleven years. I want to know who his friends were so I can look them up. I want to know what he read, how he spent his time. Who may have visited him or written to him, or to whom he may have written or telephoned while he was at the hospital. I want to know what his personality was and how he impressed people. And please do not spare my feeling on any of it because nothing but the truth, however unpleasant, can help me."

"I understand, doctor. I—I hardly know where to begin, though; you're asking so many questions at once." Dr. Magus sighed deeply. It had been the most beautiful song and dance he had ever performed. A long one, but worth it. It had convinced and it covered his asking every question he could possibly think of to ask.

He said, "Please start at the beginning, the night he was brought in. Wait, before you start and lest I forget to ask this later, is there anything you can tell me about the man he was with? A Mr. Flack, I believe the name was, also a carnival employee. Did he reach the hospital alive and if so, did he, ah, say, anything before he died, about the accident or about anything else?"

"He died after admittance to the hospital, doctor. But only minutes after and he never regained consciousness. A mercy, considering how terrible his injuries were."

"I see. And my son—was he conscious when admitted?"

"No, but he regained consciousness shortly after. While Dr. Kramer was examining him, just after the policemen left."

"The police brought him there?"

"Our own ambulance brought him, but on a call from the police. Here's how it happened that way. A state police car with two-way radio happened to be right behind the car Mr. Flack was driving and the policemen saw the accident happen. They had to slam on brakes to keep from being part of it. They radioed right in to headquarters for an ambulance—but the police ambulance was out on another call and ours was much nearer anyway so they phoned us to send our ambulance."

"I see. And John wasn't conscious when he was brought in. How soon did he recover consciousness?"

"About the time Dr. Kramer was finishing his examination and taking care of minor injuries first before setting the leg, which was the only serious injury."

"I promised not to ask about medical details, but wouldn't he have taken care of the serious injury first?"

"Oh no, not in that case. There were quite a few minor cuts from glass that were still bleeding, and a wound that's still bleeding takes priority. There's no immediate rush about setting a broken leg when it isn't a compound fracture. And—oh, yes, I remember a minor complication; there was a fairly severe cut on the leg itself at a place where it would have to be covered by the cast. Naturally that had to be taken care of first and the doctor had to be extremely sure that bleeding was completely stopped and wouldn't start again and that there wouldn't be any infection before he could put the cast on. He didn't put the leg in a cast until the next day; that night he just set it and used splints."

"What did John say when he regained consciousness?"

"Mostly, I'm afraid, he just used profanity."

"He asked no questions?"

"Oh yes, of course. As soon as he calmed down, he asked the usual questions—how bad his injuries were and how long he'd be in the hospital. He seemed very disturbed when he was told it would probably be six to eight weeks."

"Didn't he ask about his companion?"

"Yes, that was his next question. And when Dr. Kramer told him Mr. Flack had died, I remember his reaction seemed strange to me at the time. He said, 'My God!' softly, in a funny kind of way. I—I can be wrong, but I got the impression that it pleased him, as though he'd just got wonderful news."

Dr. Magus nodded. Damn right Mack Irby had just got wonderful news, he thought; he'd just learned that all the loot from that bank robbery, the whole forty-two grand, was his. Not just a cut of it, all of it. And it would have taken more than the pain of a broken leg to keep him from being quiet and doing some heavy thinking after that.

And Dr. Magus had something already—confirmation or at least a strong indication, that one of his deductions had been correct, that the money, wherever it was, hadn't been divided up as yet. If it had been, neither would have let the other know where he'd stashed his share and news of Charlie's death wouldn't have had that effect on Mack.

He said, "Thank you; Miss Plackett. I see that you are very observant. It is little things like that which are most helpful; even though I do not see their significance now, I hope to learn. When I reach the carnival, I'll inquire closely into the relations between my son and this Charles Flack. But go on."

"I'm not sure you understand, Dr. Irby. It's easy to misinterpret a tone of voice, to read something into it that isn't there, especially when a man is in shock and in pain. But that's the impression I had at the time."

"Did he ever mention Charles Flack again?"

"Not that I know of, all the time he was with us. His main worry, the first few weeks, was as to whether he could get back to the carnival before its tour ended."

"Did he ever say why that was important to him?"

"Yes, when I asked him. He said that if he didn't get back before the season ended he wouldn't be able to line himself up a job for next year."

Dr. Magus nodded gravely and inwardly exulted. It looked more and more as though the money must be with the carnival. Mack Irby, with even his own share of the bank loot, would not have been in the slightest degree interested in lining himself up a job for next season.

"His feeling that way," Miss Plackett said, "led to one definite advantage for us and for him. It made him an excellent and co-operative patient. He could, though, have left us a week earlier had he been willing to do so on crutches. But he was doing so well by then that when he learned he'd be able to walk within a week—as long as he limited his walking—with only the aid of a cane, he took the doctor's advice and waited. Of course he was sure by then that even in that case he'd get back well before the carnival ended its tour. Two weeks before, I believe."

Of course he wouldn't be in a hurry, Dr. Magus thought, once he was sure he would be back in ample time. Besides, the insurance company was paying his expenses, and Mack Irby would have hated showing up on crutches.

"I see," said Dr. Magus. "Did my son receive any mail while he was here, or send any?"

"He didn't receive any. I know because the police who were here asking about him Tuesday had me check that with the desk and with the other nurses. And as far as any of us can remember he sent out only one piece of mail, a postcard, about a week before he left. He gave it to one of the nurses, Miss Carger, to mail for him and all she remembers about it is that it was addressed to someone at the carnival."

That would have been the postcard he'd sent Burt, the one that had spread news of the insurance company's settlement around the lot.

Dr. Magus said, "Doesn't sound as though he had many friends, I'm afraid. Any telephone calls, telegrams?"

"No telegrams. One telephone call, only it wasn't exactly to him. The morning after the accident someone—What's the name of the carnival, Dr. Irby? Do you know?"

"Yes. Wiggins and Braddock Combined Shows."

"Wiggins, that's the name. I knew it was part of the name of the carnival. Anyway, the call was from Mr. Wiggins and he wanted to inquire about Mr. Irby's condition, whether it was anything serious and whether he'd be back. Dr. Kramer took the call."

"And told him what?"

She looked at him a bit strangely and he realized that the question had sounded peculiar. She said, "Told him the truth, I presume. That Mr. Irby's only serious injury was a broken leg and that he'd probably be released in six to eight weeks."

"I just wondered if he sent any messages, condolences or what not, to my son."

"Why, I don't know. Come to think of it, he probably would have left some message, to wish him good luck at least. But Dr. Kramer, if that was the case, no doubt gave the message direct to Mr. Irby."

"I see. Visitors? I suppose not, or you'd have mentioned the fact already."

"No, no one came to see him, unless you count the insurance adjuster. He came twice, the second time to bring the check for the settlement they made."

Dr. Magus frowned thoughtfully. "I'm afraid that doesn't give me many leads. I'd hoped to find out who his friends were, but apparently he hadn't many. Well, he thought enough of someone at the carnival at least to send a postcard. And I'll no doubt be able to find out who that was when I reach the carnival. Uh, what was his attitude toward money? In particular, before he knew for certain that there would be an easy settlement with the insurance company, including covering his hospital bill."

"Why, he didn't seem to worry about it. Naturally we check with a patient, since we're not a charity institution, as to whether or not he's going to be able to pay our bill. In the case of an emergency admittance like Mr. Irby's we do it, of course, after emergency treatment has been given. In Mr. Irby's case, the hospital superintendent talked to him about it the following day. I happened to be in the room. Let's see, I'll try to remember as much of the conversation as I can."

She closed her eyes. "Dr. Harper, that's the superintendent's name, asked him first—I guess it's always the first question—whether he carried hospitalization or accident insurance, and Mr. Irby said he didn't. Dr. Harper then told him that if his hospitalization ran eight weeks the total bill would be close to a thousand dollars and that he'd have to pay it in cash before he could be released, and that if he didn't have that much money he should ask then to be transferred to a county institution. And Mr. Irby said—I think I remember exactly what he said—'That's all right, doc. Don't let it worry you.'"

Dr. Magus nodded happily, his face grave. Not that he needed more proof of Irby's being in the bank robbery, but there it was. At the time Miss Plackett was telling about, Irby's winter stake had been nine hundred and fifty in postal savings and a little over a hundred in cash, yet he hadn't even thought twice about agreeing to use almost all of it to pay a hospital bill. And before he knew—at least before he could be certain—that he had a settlement coming from the company that had issued liability insurance to the driver of the other car.

Money, to the tune of almost a thousand dollars he might have had to pay himself, hadn't counted, against the importance of getting the best of care and treatment so he could get back to the carnival before the season ended. And leave himself without a winter stake just so he could make a connection for next season? Nuts, Mack Irby was a good enough talker that he could have made a connection any time he wanted to.

"I see," he said again. Well, he'd done pretty well, he figured. He was now completely certain Mack had had the forty-two grand. He was reasonably certain now that it was with the carnival. The time and expense of his trip to Glenrock had been worth while. But there was still a random possibility that he might get more.

He smiled sadly. "I'm afraid, Miss Plackett, that I've just about run out of specific questions. Suppose you just tell me anything more that you may remember about him, or things he said or did, however unimportant or irrelevant it may seem to you. It is just possible—Did he ever say anything that might have the slightest bearing on his childhood, for example?"

He hadn't, but she thought of and told him throughout the rest of dinner a hundred little things. None was remotely relevant. It was over dessert that Dr. Magus thought of the question he should have asked first of all.

"Ah—Miss Plackett, was his leg set under a general or a local anesthetic?"

"A general, Sodium Pentothal. He was still suffering somewhat from shock and still in pain from cuts and bruises so Dr. Kramer decided on a general anesthetic.

"Do not people often talk deliriously when they are coming out of an anesthetic? Sometimes nonsense, of course, but such nonsense as can come from things that are deep in their subconscious minds, things that are desperately important to them."

"Yes, doctor. And Mr. Irby did rave a bit when he was coming out. But I'm afraid that it was all in the nonsense category, to me, and that I don't remember any of it." Dr. Magus leaned earnestly forward. "Will you try very hard to remember, my dear? It's just possible that even a phrase or word of that seeming nonsense would refer back to his childhood, would mean something to me, would give me the very key I am searching for."

"I'll try my best, doctor. Let me think." She paused, staring off into space. "Some of it was swearing—I remember the word, 'Jeez,' a corruption of 'Jesus,' I suppose. And—and there was a number, but I can't remember what the number was."

Dr. Magus found that he was holding his breath; he had to let it out carefully before he could speak. He said softly. "I wonder—I punished him once, when he was about six years old, for using that very word, 'Jeez,' Miss Plackett. I didn't think of the punishment as being a severe one but—just possibly it was one that affected him psychologically more severely than I suspected. I temporarily deprived him of some toy soldiers he was very fond of. I believe there were, ah, forty-two of them."

"That's the number, doctor! He'd say, 'Forty-two, Jeez!' and then laugh. He said that several times. Oh, doctor, I do hope that's helpful. And I see now what you mean about things that sounded like nonsense to me being important to you. There was another phrase—" She stared into space again. Dr. Magus didn't move a muscle.

"Something about pickles," she said. "No, it was pickle punks, or pickled punks. And something about 'it,' whatever 'it' was, being stuffed in a two-headed calf."

Dr. Magus let himself relax very slowly. His head was swimming a little; he didn't trust his voice for a moment. Then he said, "I'm sorry, but I'm afraid that doesn't mean anything to me either. But the swear word and the oblique reference to the toy soldiers may be very valuable. I'll think about it and try to follow it farther. Thank you very much, my dear. And may we finish this delightful meal with a spot of brandy?"

Champagne would have been better, magnums of champagne, for forty-two thousand wonderful reasons. But alas that would have been out of character for a professor in search of the reason for his son's waywardness.

But he could and did insist on the best brandy they had, and he could and did touch his brandy glass to hers and say, "To you, Miss Plackett, with my deepest gratitude."

And his smile was beautiful.

CHAPTER TWENTY-ONE

Sammy wandered lonely as a cloud. Jesse had knocked off a little early, just early enough to be sure of getting a seat in the poker game that was starting in the G-top.

And now the model show had closed, the unborn show had closed, the merry-go-round and most of the other shows had closed. Only the hanky panks and the grab joint and a few other things that didn't take much extra overhead to keep operating still ran to get a few more dimes or quarters from the few marks who still hung around the midway.

Sammy wandered once around outside the tops and then once around the midway, not knowing quite what to do with himself. If only Mr. Evans wasn't mad at him! But he was, and now he was afraid of Mr. Evans.

Mr. Evans might hit him again if he even asked to see those books. And he wanted to see those pictures again, especially the ones in that big expensive-looking book, the first one he'd looked at. He remembered what the simpler ones of those pictures were like, but the others were getting foggy in his mind and he wanted to see them again.

He walked slowly, trying to remember. Someone behind him said, "Hello, Sammy."

Sammy turned and his face brightened with a smile. "Hi, Mr. Magus." He saw that Mr. Magus looked happy, very very happy. There was a gentle smile on his face, but the real happiness showed in his eyes. It made Sammy feel good all over to look at Mr. Magus's eyes. He liked to see people happy. He said, "Gee, you look purty, Mr. Magus." Purty, or even pretty, wasn't exactly the word he wanted but it was the only word he could think of. Besides the happiness, there was the way Mr. Magus was dressed; he'd never seen Mr. Magus all dressed up like he was now. "Gee, the way you're all dressed up."

Mr. Magus put a finger to his lips and leaned forward confidentially. "Don't tell anyone, Sammy, but I'm to be Queen of the May."

"What's that, Mr. Magus?"

"It is a consummation most devoutly to be wished for. Sammy, I have a thought. There is welling up within me the desire to talk, and it occurs to me that you are the perfect audience for the occasion. In fact, you are the one and only person in this tinseled charnel house to whom I may, within reasonable limits, unburden myself. Will you listen to me?"

"Sure, Mr. Magus. Gee, I am listening to you."

"Ah, yes. But under better and more relaxed circumstances. In the privacy of my little mitt camp and over a flagon of—Do you drink, Sammy?"

"Not much, Mr. Magus. Jesse lets me have a drink once in a while. Once I had three but it made me feel funnylike. I like cotton candy better."

"Ah, cotton candy. Is the booth still open?"

"Gee, I don't know. I can see if it is."

Mr. Magus reached in his pocket and took out a fifty-cent piece. "Go see if it is, Sammy."

"Spend all of this?"

"By all means, if your stomach will stand the gaff." Sammy raced to the booth. The Cotton Candy Lady was just closing but when he showed her the money and told her he wanted five cones of cotton candy, she sighed and turned the machine back on and poured more pink sugar into it. He ate the first cone of it while she was making the other four.

He raced back. The light was on inside the mitt camp. He called out Mr. Magus's name and Mr. Magus called, "Come in, Sammy."

Mr. Magus had his coat and tie off. He'd spread a blanket on the ground and was sitting on it leaning back against the foot locker. A whisky bottle stood on the little table where he could reach up and get it easily.

"Pull up a corner of blanket and sit down, Sammy," he said.

Sammy sat down, but Mr. Magus just sat looking at him, not talking like he said he was going to talk at all, just looking at Sammy. Mr. Magus looked like he was thinking hard.

Sammy ate cotton candy and it was good, but he kept wishing Mr. Magus would start talking. He didn't always understand much of what Mr. Magus said, but he liked the smooth sound of his voice.

But he finished two more cones of cotton candy before Mr. Magus spoke at all. Then he asked a question. "Sammy, could I trust you to do something for me and never tell anyone?"

"Gee, sure. Anything, Mr. Magus."

"You won't even tell Jesse?" Mr. Magus wasn't smiling.

"Not even tell Jesse. If you say not, Mr. Magus."

"I say not. And I believe you, Sammy. Listen now, and I'll explain it to you. Listen carefully. I'll try to use all words that you understand and you concentra . . . you think hard. First, you know Barney King, don't you? He's talker for the unborn show."

Sammy nodded. "I know Mr. King."

Mr. Magus spoke very slowly. "I want to play a joke on Mr. King, Sammy. Just a joke, but I don't want him to know about it or to know I did it. Do you understand?"

"Yes, Mr. Magus. You want to play a joke on Mr. King."

"Right. Now, Sammy, just before I met you on the midway I'd looked in the G-top and Mr. King was playing poker there. In a few minutes now, after you finish that God-awful mess of cotton candy you're eating, we'll go out together and you'll wait till I look in the G-top and make sure Mr. King is still playing. I can't play the joke on him unless he's still there. Understand so far, Sammy?"

Sammy nodded and stuffed more cotton candy into his mouth.

"If he is, we'll walk down to the unborn show. And you wait in front. You lean against the ticket booth and watch back toward the direction of the G-top, where Mr. King will be. You watch while I go around to the side of the top and under the canvas. Mr. King sleeps there, inside the unborn show top, in a bed roll, and that's where I'm going to get the joke ready for him. Still with me, Sammy?"

"Yes, Mr. Magus. I wait outside and watch while you go in to play a joke on Mr. King."

"Good boy. And while I'm in there—it will be only a few minutes—you watch and if you see Mr. King coming back, you start to sing."

"Sing what, Mr. Magus?"

"Sing anything. Any song you know. You can sing, can't you?"

"Yes, Mr. Magus. I can sing 'Three Blind Mice' and—"

"That will be fine, Sammy. If you see Mr. King coming, you sing 'Three Blind Mice'—or if you forget that sing anything, just so you sing loud enough that I'll be sure to hear you. This is very important, Sammy. All right, you're through with that damn floss candy now. Lick off your fingers and let's get going."

Mr. Magus took a flashlight from the foot locker and put it in his pocket, then went out.

Sammy followed him to the G-top but waited outside because if he went in Jesse would see him and might tell him to go to sleep and quit wandering around and he didn't want to go to sleep now because after he stood watch for Mr. Magus, Mr. Magus might still talk to him like he said he was going to. Mr. Magus came out and said, "Okay, Sammy, he's still playing."

He followed Mr. Magus to the front of the unborn show. Mr. Magus showed him just where to stand and which way to watch—as though he didn't know that. Then he asked, "And if you see Mr. King coming, what are you going to do?"

"Sing 'Three Blind Mice,' real loud."

"That's my boy, Sammy. And then, after you've sung it, you go back to the mitt camp. I'll be there already, around the back way. Now you don't think about anything else. You just watch and be ready to sing."

Mr. Magus patted him on the arm and disappeared into the shadows.

Mr. King didn't come.

After a few minutes Mr. Magus was there beside him again. He said, "Good work, Sammy. Thanks a lot. And now you're going to forget all about this. You're not even going to tell Jesse. It just never happened. Right, Sammy?"

"Sure, Mr. Magus."

"You see, the joke wouldn't be funny if Mr. King ever learned, from anybody, that I'd been there tonight. And now let's go back to my place."

"Do you still want to talk to me, Mr. Magus?"

"Try me and see, Sammy."

And then they were back in the mitt camp, sitting as they were before. Dr. Magus picked up the whisky bottle and grinned at Sammy. He handed it across. "Have one, Sammy. In fact, have the three Jesse allows you, but not all at once. Only remember this—he didn't tell you exactly how big those brinies could be. So take a long one."

Sammy took a long one, and it almost choked him and made his eyes water. But even so it tasted so much better and so much smoother that he didn't mind it as much. He looked at the bottle and saw that it was different; it had paper on it, a label; the color was darker. He looked at the label again before he passed it back. He asked, "What does it say on there, Mr. Magus?"

Mr. Magus smiled "What it says is irrelevant, Sammy. What it should say is just two words, Drink Me, in big type. Have you ever read—had read to you—Alice in Wonderland and Through the Looking Glass?"

And Mr. Magus looked genuinely shocked when Sammy said he'd never heard of them. "Have they got pitchers in them?" he asked.

"Yes, they have pictures. Very good drawings. But it's the stories that really matter. I wish I had one of them here, Sammy; I'm in just the mood to read aloud from Lewis Carroll. But about the label on the bottle. It's in the first book and Alice finds it just after she gets down the rabbit hole. She finds a bottle with a label that says Drink Me and a cake with a tag that says Eat Me. But Lewis Carroll, the man who wrote the stories, had the labels mixed because when Alice drank from the bottle it made her smaller and eating the cake made her bigger again.

"But Mr. Carroll got that wrong because he wasn't really Mr. Carroll at all; he was a minister named Dodgson, and a teetotaler, so he didn't understand about drinking. Only small men drink, Sammy—but so many of us are small men. Small men drink because drinking makes them bigger for a while and frees them from the bitter knowledge of how small they are. For a while, no matter how short a while, they can stride like giants, reach for stars. It's all illusion, yes, but who can say the dull world of sobriety is not also an illusion, and certainly a less happy one. Do you not agree?"

Sammy said, "Gee, Mr. Magus, I dunno." But he didn't really care because he liked the sound of Mr. Magus's voice and he liked the roll and march of the strange words. But there was something he wanted to know. "Tell me some more about my being rich, Mr. Magus."

"Your being . . . Oh, yes, Sammy. Well, there isn't much to tell except that you will be. And what will you do with your money? Besides, of course, buying a cotton candy spinner and hiring an expert operator to run it for you."

"Gee, I dunno. I guess maybe I'd get myself a woman."

Mr. Magus's eyes widened. "Haven't you ever had a woman, Sammy?"

Sammy shook his head. "But I know how, Mr. Magus. I seen pitchers. Mr. Evans's got books with pitchers and I seen them, honest. Only now Mr. Evans doesn't like me any more and won't let me look at them. Do you have any pitchers like that?"

"Some very lovely ones, Sammy. But only in my mind. I fear I cannot show them to you."

"Why can't you show them to me, Mr. Magus?"

"As I told you, Sammy, they are in my mind. Don't you have some pictures in your mind? Of course you have. Close your eyes and think of—of the merry-go-round. Doesn't a picture of it come into your head?" Sammy nodded.

Mr. Magus's eyes twinkled at him. "Why can't you show it to me, Sammy?"

Sammy grinned and didn't answer. But he understood now what Mr. Magus had meant.

"You see, Sammy, those are the best kinds of pictures to have. You can't lose them and nobody can take them away from you. Only people whose minds can't hold pictures for them want pornographic pictures to look at. Pictures in the mind are better by far because they are things one has already experienced and can re-experience by remembering them—and with tactile sensations as well as merely visual ones."

"But how can I get pitchers like that, Mr. Magus?"

"There is only one way, Sammy. But, ah, I fear I do see practical difficulties in your case, not insurmountable ones—no difficulty and few women are completely insurmountable—and yet—" Mr. Magus stared darkly at the bottle and then handed it over to Sammy wordlessly. Sammy drank from it and handed it back.

Sammy said, "But when I'm rich like you say I'm gonna be, with paper money, then I can have a woman. Mr. King, he told me that's what I'd need"

"Mr. King has a point there. I had not thought of that possibility, being personally prejudiced against the commercialization of such transactions. But granting them to be better than no transactions at all, which I freely grant—yes, Sammy, in your particular case Mr. King indubitably has a point. But if—I mean when you become rich you must be careful in deciding what woman to offer paper money to. Some would slap you in the face and some would call copper. You sound as though you've been thinking seriously about this, Sammy."

"Gee, I have, Mr. Magus. About Miss Trixie. I like Miss Trixie a lot and Mr. King said she'd do it for paper money. She wouldn't slap me or call copper, would she?"

"Ummm, a most fortunate choice, in a way. Your own instincts and Barney King's advice are equally good I am tempted, I am very strongly tempted—"

Mr. Magus took a billfold out of his hip pocket and took a piece of paper money from it, stared at the money.

"Is this a tenner that I see before me?" Then he sighed and put the money back. "No, Sammy, it would be wrong for me to give you that money. For me to give you money for that purpose would be playing God. And I am too small a man, even in my cups, to play God."

He took another drink, a long one, from the bottle. "You see, Sammy, there are factors involved not even my madball could tell me. There is Jesse. While I do not personally approve of Jesse's, uh, philosophy, there is the undeniable fact that because of it you have a degree of security that would be impossible for you to have otherwise, outside the confines of an institution. You were in an institution before Jesse found you, weren't you?"

"I was in a place, Mr. Magus. They kept me there. I guess it was an ins—what you said."

"And you didn't like it?"

"I hated it. I ran away. I like here better, the carney."

"And by giving you money I might be jeopardizing your chances of staying here. It might lead to either of two things—Jesse learning about it and kicking you out, as he might, or you yourself deciding to run away from Jesse. Sammy, all my humanitarian and Pindarean instincts tell me that all is nothing beside the fact that you are apparently ready for a great experiment and that it should not be denied you, whatever the consequences. Yet I am stopped by the ugly specter of my common sense which tells me— what it tells me."

"You mean you don't think I should have a woman?"

"I did not say that, Sammy. Please remember that I did not say that. I mean only that I do not believe in omniscience, even my own. Get thee behind me,

Sammy. And hie thee hence that I may Morpheus woo. Good night."

"Good night, Mr. Magus. And thanks for the cotton candy and everything."

Lonely as a cloud, Sammy wandered. The midway was dark now except for the few bulbs that burned all night. His stomach felt warm from the drinks he'd had from Mr. Magus's bottle and his head felt light. And it had been wonderful having Mr. Magus talk for so long, just to him. Despite the loneliness of the deserted lot he felt almost happy now, almost satisfied to be alone.

It was so nice that Mr. Magus would talk to him and not care whether he understood or not. Other people weren't like that. If Jesse said something to him and he didn't understand, Jesse got awful mad. Most other people got impatient. Only Mr. Magus didn't mind at all.

It came to him that maybe, this late, Jesse was back in their quarters and getting mad because he wasn't there, so Sammy walked to the G-top and listened outside it until he heard Jesse's voice and knew Jesse was still playing cards.

He was still standing there in the shadow of the G-top, still with his ear near the canvas, when he saw Miss Trixie. She was walking fast, away from him. He wondered where she was going and stepped out of the shadow so he could follow her with his eyes. She went toward the trailer, Mr. Evans's trailer. She rapped on the door. A light went on inside and the door opened. Miss Trixie went in and the door closed behind her.

Just a few days ago Sammy would have thought she was going there just to talk to Mr. Evans and maybe have a drink with him. But Sammy had learned a lot since then. He knew about women now and what some of them did, and he knew Miss Trixie was one of the ones who did it.

He wondered if they'd let him watch. That would be better than looking at the pictures again. That would give him pictures in his mind and Mr. Magus had just told him those were the best kind and that if he had pictures in his mind he wouldn't want to look at pictures on paper.

But then he remembered that Mr. Evans was mad at him and had hit him. And might hit him again if he even went there to ask if he could watch.

The shades on the windows of the trailer were being pulled down now but one of them, the one just to the left of the door, didn't go quite all the way down; there was still a crack of light between it and the bottom of the window. Maybe he could see through there and watch and Mr. Evans wouldn't even know he was watching.

Sammy tiptoed over.

He hoped he wouldn't have to stand there too long because the night had turned chilly and he was shivering.

The bottom of the trailer window was at the level of his chest; he had to bend down a bit to put his eyes to the crack. At first he couldn't see anything except the edge of the bunk and the wall past the bunk. Then Miss Trixie walked into view. She still had all her clothes on except for the coat she'd been wearing on her way to the trailer. At his angle of vision he could see only from her knees to her breasts. Then she sat down on the bunk, facing his way, and he could see her face too.

Then Mr. Evans came into view. He had an old bathrobe on. Sammy remembered the trailer had been dark until Miss Trixie had knocked; Mr. Evans must have been in bed and put the bathrobe on when he got up to turn on the light and let her in. But why had Mr. Evans put on clothes instead of Miss Trixie taking hers off? Maybe Miss Trixie had come just to talk after all. Then Sammy saw that Mr. Evans had a drink in each hand, two drinks altogether, and he handed one to Miss Trixie and sat down beside her. Maybe they were just going to have a drink first and then do some of the things like in those pictures in Mr. Evans's books.

Sammy shivered again and wondered if he had time to go back and get his jacket. But he might miss something if he did. And what Mr. Evans did next showed Sammy that there would be something to miss all right. He sat farther back on the bunk than Miss Trixie was sitting, leaned back against the wall. He held his drink in his left hand and his right hand reached behind Miss Trixie and Sammy could tell that it was unbuttoning buttons at the back of her dress. Then his hand pulled her back to lean against him and slid inside the front of her dress.

Suddenly Sammy sneezed.

The sneeze was not only a loud one but it was so unexpected that it made his head jerk forward; his forehead hit the pane of the window with a resounding thump, so painfully as almost to blind him for a second.

He turned and ran for the concealing shadow of the G-top, but he'd taken only a few steps when he heard the door jerk open behind him and he knew Mr. Evans was seeing him run, recognizing him even from behind at so short a distance, in the moonlight.

But no footsteps came running after him and he paused and waited in the shadow of the canvas. He stood there panting, wondering what he should do, or if he should do anything at all. Mr. Evans hadn't run after him, hadn't even called out at him, so maybe it was all right. Maybe Mr. Evans hadn't minded and it would be all right for him to go back and watch as long as he didn't sneeze and bump the window again.

But while he was wondering the door of the trailer opened again and Mr. Evans came out. He'd put on a shirt and trousers and he started walking, but not toward Sammy. After a few steps Sammy could see that he was heading around for the other side of the G-top, where the entrance was.

He was going to tell Jesse on Sammy. And that meant that what Sammy had done, looking in the window, had been something awful bad.

Sammy whirled and ran, as far as the edge of the lot. But he stopped there. Where could he run to?

That was the edge of the world, his world. He crossed it only to run an errand for someone and then just to some grocery store or drug store that was in sight of the lot or that someone had told him how to find only a block or two away. And then he always watched carefully just how he was going and concentrated so he could find his way back.

But at night? If he once got out of sight of the carnival he'd probably never be able to find it again and it would move on to another town and he'd be back like he was before Jesse found him, with nothing to eat, and finally the cops would pick him up and put him back in a place with bars on the windows and a high wall around the yard and this time they wouldn't let him get away. They'd have learned, and this time wouldn't leave a door open for him.

No, he couldn't run away. There was nowhere to run to.

He'd just have to go back and take whatever beating Jesse was going to give him. And it would be a bad one. He knew now, although he still didn't know why, looking in that window must have been a really bad thing to do. Otherwise Mr. Evans might have done something about it himself but he wouldn't have gone to Jesse about it.

A step at a time he made himself go back toward the midway. He gave Mr. Evans's trailer a wide berth and headed straight for the sleeping top. He stood outside it, trembling, wondering if Jesse was inside, waiting for him. He thought of sleeping somewhere else tonight, in one of the trucks or under one of the bally platforms in the freak show top where he and Jesse usually slept when Jesse had rented the sleeping top to someone for all night.

But that would make Jesse madder, if he didn't show up to take his beating. Tomorrow Jesse would have two things to beat him for and it would be better to take one beating tonight and have it over with than to have two beatings tomorrow.

He took a deep breath and went in. Jesse wasn't there. It was pitch dark inside but he could tell right away that Jesse wasn't there yet because he could have heard Jesse breathing even if Jesse hadn't spoken.

He groped until he found the little carbide lantern and some matches and got it lighted. By its light he sat and waited. He didn't dare undress and get into bed because if he was naked Jesse's blows would hurt worse.

He put his jacket on so he wouldn't sneeze any more and then sat on top of the bedding, waiting.

Finally Jesse came.

He crawled through the flap and stood up just inside, his head bent to clear the canvas, looking down at Sammy. He was sober but his eyes were cold and hard.

"Get out," he said.

Sammy pulled back. He whimpered. Jesse couldn't really be sending him away for good.

Jesse said, "I'm through with you."

"But Jesse—please. What did I do?"

"Don't matter what you done. I wasn't gonna feed you all winter anyhow and it might's well be now as end of season. Before you get in trouble that gets me in too. Finding bodies, dirty pictures, Peeping Tom stuff. No more halfwit angelinos for me. Get out."

Jesse didn't want him any more. He stared up at Jesse's face, too stupefied to move.

Jesse said, "Goddam it, get out right now or I'll beat hell out of you."

Jesse stepped aside a little, just far enough that Sammy could get out past him. He took off his belt, the heavy one he always wore and that he sometimes beat Sammy with, and held it in his hand ready to swing. Buckle end down.

Sammy looked at the buckle and whimpered again. Then he crawled out through the tent flap past Jesse.

Out into the night, the lonely night bright with moonlight and dark with dread.

CHAPTER TWENTY-TWO

Saturday morning. Dr. Magus woke early, knowing he had a big day ahead of him.

He'd better operate the mitt camp, for one thing, lest people start wondering why he was working so little. And besides that he had certain preparations to make. None of them difficult but all of them important.

Last night while Sammy had kept watch for him outside the unborn show he'd given the jar that contained the two-headed calf fetus as careful an examination as he could with the flashlight. It was a wide-mouthed five-gallon jar. Pretty heavy, but he could manage to get it from the unborn show to the mitt camp and back again. Forty-two thousand dollars lighter on the way back. But he'd want an empty cardboard carton to carry it in; a five-gallon jar looks too much like a five-gallon jar, even wrapped in canvas, for him to risk being seen carrying it. And it would be easier to carry if he roped the carton shut so he could carry it by the rope. Item one, a cardboard carton the right size to hold the jar. Item two, rope.

Item three, rubber cement. His study of the fetus through the glass of the jar had convinced him that it was a hollow rubber fake. It would have to be, anyway, to be the hiding place for the money. Flack and Irby would never have thought of gutting and stuffing a real fetus; it would be a horribly messy thing to do. They'd never have been able to do it undetectably, either. And a real fetus would be in formaldehyde, which is horrible stuff; even if they'd protected themselves with gas masks the odor would have advertised what they were doing all over the lot. Irby, as talker for Burt, must have known in advance and for sure that the fetus was hollow rubber and in water. And they'd have sealed the slit they made, not only to keep the money dry but because water getting in would lower the level of water in the jar and show evidence of tampering. He'd need rubber cement to reseal it for the same reason.

Razor blades he already had, plenty of them.

So much for shopping. He'd go into town this morning and take care of it.

So much for means. Opportunity was going to be a tougher nut to crack. Barney King spread his bedroll in the unborn show top and slept there. And he not only had to take that jar away but take it back afterwards. He might be able to do the whole operation in half an hour but he couldn't count on it. He wanted to make sure Barney would be safely away from his sleeping quarters for at least a couple of hours.

Furthermore, he very much wanted those two hours to be tonight. Tomorrow night there'd be no chance; tomorrow night was Sunday night and tear-down; packing and moving would start even before the carnival had closed. And what if that jar got broken in transit! Of course it had been moved from lot to lot all season without breaking—six of those times since it had become the repository of the loot from the bank— but he'd worry like hell about it just the same. And the suspense of waiting at least two more nights would be unendurable.

It had to be tonight He'd have to figure out something that would take Barney King off the lot tonight after the show closed. A song and dance for that shouldn't be too difficult, with a little money—not enough to arouse suspicion—for bait.

He figured it out on his way into town on the bus. Groundwork consisted only in making a few telephone calls for information and then sending himself a telegram at the lot, specifying that it was to be delivered and not telephoned there.

When he got back he stashed his purchases at the mitt camp and wandered to the office wagon to see if there was any mail for him.

"Nope, Doc, no mail," Smitty told him, "but there's a telegram. Here it is."

Dr. Magus tore open the envelope and pretended to read it, then swore.

"Bad news, Doc?"

"Not bad news, no. But my brother's coming to see me, wants my help on a deal, and he wants me to meet him at some airport with a car at one o'clock tonight. And I'll be busy then—a big deal of my own on the fire."

"Get somebody to meet him for you."

"I believe I can do that. Thanks, Smitty."

Dr. Magus wandered to the unborn show and called Barney's name from outside the canvas, then ducked under it when Barney called back for him to come in.

Barney was putting on his talking clothes. "How's every little thing, Doc?" he asked.

"Not too bad. Barney, does your jalopy still run?"

"Yep."

"Wonder if you could use it to do me a favor."

Barney looked at his wrist watch. "Burt said we'd open at two today and it's half past one now. If it's a short trip—"

"It isn't. It's rather a long one. But it's tonight after closing, not now. And it's quite a favor if you can do it for me, too big a favor to ask for free. There's a sawbuck in it, besides your gas."

"A sawbuck I could use. What's the deal?"

"I just got a telegram, Barney. My brother's coming to see me on business. And he's flying into the Springer airport late tonight—guess either Bloomfield hasn't got an airport or he couldn't make connections for it." Dr. Magus sat down on the corner of a table lined with glass jars and took the telegram from his pocket and looked at it as though to refresh himself on the details. "Here is the hell of it. He might be on either of two planes and won't know which till he takes off. There's one in at one-forty and—will you be able to make it? How late's Burt likely to want to run the show tonight?"

"Not much after midnight, if any. How's the distance? How far is Springer from here?"

"Forty miles, but it's on the same main highway. You can make it, can't you?"

"Sure, easy. I can leave here by half past twelve and make it easy. What's this about another plane, though?"

"If he isn't on that one-forty plane you'll have to wait fifty minutes for the other one. It's in at half past two. I fear the round trip plus the wait between the planes— if he isn't on the first one, of course—will take you about three hours."

"That's all right, Doc. No plans tonight anyway And I can sure use ten bucks after what the poker game did to me last night. Yeah, half past twelve will be okay for us to take off. Where'll we meet."

Dr. Magus shook his head. "I can't go, Barney. I've got a deal on. Business. A séance."

"A séance? You mean ghost stuff? I didn't know you went in for that, Doc."

"I don't ordinarily. But when a mark I was giving a good reading to a few days ago asked me about a séance I didn't tell her that. I just told her the fee was fifty bucks and she surprised the hell out of me by taking me up on it."

"I'll be damned. But after midnight?"

Dr. Magus nodded. "This is the anniversary of her husband's death, or will be at two o'clock tonight. She wants a séance in the room he died in, right at that hour. She's going to pick me up in her car at one o'clock."

Barney King shivered a little. "That fifty bucks I wouldn't want to earn. Dunno if I believe in ghosts or not but I sure as hell wouldn't want to try to raise one at that time of night in the room he died in."

Dr. Magus chuckled. "I can handle any ghosts I raise myself. But just in case this one gets me, I'll pay you now, Barney. Here's the ten and—let's see, what will cover gas and oil for forty miles each way?"

"Couple bucks ought to cover it."

"Let's make it three."

"Thanks. Say, how do I know this guy, your brother?"

"Looks like me; you can't miss him. He's about an inch taller, six years younger, no goatee. But there's enough resemblance that you can't possibly miss it. And you can level with him as to why I can't meet him. He'll understand. Half a C is half a C and this one is tonight or never."

"Shall I take him to the mitt camp?"

"If he wants to wait for me there. Leave it up to him, Barney. If he'd rather stay at a hotel drop him off at one and tell him I'll see him first thing in the morning."

"Okay, Doc. About whether he should wait for you or not—is there any chance you might be gone all night? Might this dame be looking for a stand-in for her husband?"

"I don't know. But she isn't bad; I might oblige her if she has that in mind, but it'll still cost her fifty bucks for the séance." He grinned. "In which, now that I think of it, I am reasonably certain that her husband will tell her to enjoy herself and not to be faithful to a memory," Dr. Magus started out and then turned back. "Should tell you one thing, Barney. My brother is pretty unpredictable. I wouldn't put it past him not to show up on either of those planes. If he isn't on the second one, don't let it worry you. Just come back and turn in."

"Sure. Hey, what's your brother's name?"

"His name is Legion. Harry J. Legion."

The afternoon was bright and warm, the evening balmy. And the double murder that had broken in the Friday papers was still fresh enough to draw the morbidly curious, who seemed to be most of the population of Bloomfield.

Dr. Magus read palms until his eyes blurred and his voice became hoarse. Money rolled in.

But time never dragged more slowly.

CHAPTER TWENTY-THREE

Sammy was hungry. It was late now and the carnival was closing, and all he'd eaten all day was one hamburger sandwich around noon, almost twelve hours ago. He was awfully hungry again now.

But no one had asked him to run any errands since noon, when Maybelle had sent him to bring her a hamburger; she'd given him half a dollar and had said, "Keep the change, Sammy, or get yourself a hamburger too." And it had been a good idea because by then he was hungry already; he wanted a hamburger more than he wanted cotton candy. Cotton candy didn't help at all when you were hungry. Sammy knew enough to know that. Cotton candy tasted wonderful but it was mostly just air; it didn't fill your stomach like solid food did.

After that hamburger, although he could have eaten two more along with it, he'd felt better for a while. It was the heat of the day then and he'd curled up under the outside bally platform of the freak show and had napped for a while; that was his sleeping place now. Anyway, it was the place where he'd slept last night after Jesse had kicked him out.

He'd slept there again from noon until the thumping of the bass drum bright over his head had wakened him and he'd crawled out and wandered around the lot hoping someone would send him on another errand and pay him for it so he could get more to eat.

But he couldn't ask. He shouldn't ever ask anybody for money or for food or even for a chance to run an errand and earn money or food. If somebody called him over and asked him to do something for them, that was all right. But never bother anybody; that was one of the things Jesse had been strictest about, never bother people asking them for money or food or candy or for errands to run. Of all the things Jesse had taught him that was the hardest one to live up to now when his stomach hurt.

But he had to live up to it now, keep from doing anything Jesse wouldn't want him to do, or there wouldn't be any chance that Jesse would take him back. And having Jesse take him back was the only answer to his problem. Jesse was his only security. Jesse was mean to him sometimes but Jesse took care of him and fed him and told him what to do and what not to do. Nobody else ever had, as far back as he could remember and he doubted that anyone else ever would.

He had to hope that Jesse would take him back.

And he'd planned carefully, so carefully, just how he'd go about getting Jesse to take him back. He'd planned it when he had awakened this morning. He'd keep out of Jesse's sight, never go past the ball game booth or let Jesse see him anywhere on the lot.

Then Jesse would think he'd gone, and be sorry.

All day he'd not once gone near the ball game booth and he hadn't gone near the chow top around the times when Jesse went there to eat. Jesse hadn't seen him once.

And he'd do the same thing tomorrow, and tomorrow was the last day in Bloomfield and that would give Jesse another day to think he was gone forever and to be sorry. But he'd be on the one of the trucks, still without Jesse having seen him, when the carney moved on from Bloomfield to the next town, whatever town it was, and there, on Monday when Jesse was setting up the booth for business in that town he'd walk up and ask Jesse if he could help. And by then Jesse would be so sorry and so glad to see him that he'd take him back. He'd remember how good and how faithful Sammy had been and he'd think how clever and smart Sammy had been to find the carnival again, even in a different town (because Jesse wouldn't know that Sammy had been with the carnival all along; he'd think Sammy had found it again in the new town). Jesse would even cry, maybe, and he'd say, "Sammy, Sammy, I'm sorry. I thought I'd lost you. I didn't really mean it at all."

Looking ahead to that, Sammy had been good all day. He'd tried his best to follow every rule Jesse had ever told him.

He'd even stayed away from Mr. Magus. Of all people on the lot Mr. Magus had probably been the nicest to him and he'd been the first person Sammy had thought of when he got so hungry. He'd even wandered near the mitt camp once during the day but Mr. Magus hadn't been there. That had been a good thing; if he had been Sammy might have weakened and asked him if he wanted an errand run and that would have been breaking Jesse's strictest rule. Because it was when he broke rules that things went wrong and if he lived by all the rules—no matter how hungry he got—nothing would go wrong and his plan would work out just as he wanted it to work out.

If only he didn't break any rules that he didn't know about yet! Like the rule against finding a body or looking in a window or any of the other things he hadn't ever known he shouldn't do until he'd done them.

Looking in a window must be just about the worst. It was because he'd done that that Jesse had kicked him out and told him to go away. Only Jesse would never have known he'd done it if Mr. Evans hadn't told on him.

He hated Mr. Evans. It was all Mr. Evans's fault that this had happened. Mr. Evans had used to be so nice to him, letting him look at the pictures in magazines and sometimes letting him run errands, and then Mr. Evans had suddenly started to be mean to him. He'd hit him and made him fall just because he'd wanted to see those books again.

Mr. Evans could just have said no without hitting him. But even hitting him hadn't been a tenth as bad as telling on him had been. Mr. Evans could just have said, "Sammy, don't look in my window," and Sammy would have gone away; he'd have known then that not looking in windows was one of the rules and he'd never have done it again. But instead Mr. Evans had told Jesse on him. It was Mr. Evans's fault he was hungry now.

Hungry and now almost without hope of being asked to do an errand tonight. The midway was all dark except for the night lights and everything was closed and there were only a few people around. He'd have to go to bed with his stomach hurting and hope people would give him errands to do tomorrow or he'd have to go hungry another day too and not eat until Jesse took him back the first day in the next town.

Someone was coming toward him. It was Mr. King.

Sammy straightened up and said, "Hi, Mr. King," hopefully. But Mr. King just said, "Hi, Sammy," and walked on past. Sammy turned and watched him. Mr. King got into his car. The engine started and the headlights went on and Mr. King drove away. Sammy was alone again.

He was near the chow top. It was still open, brightly lighted. It always stayed open an hour or two after the carnival closed so the carneys could get something to eat before they turned in for the night. There were people in there; he could hear their voices.

Worse, he could smell food. Hamburgers frying, the smell of coffee. His mouth watered a little.

Suddenly Jesse came out of the chow top.

Sammy turned to run but Jesse yelled "Hey!" and Sammy waited. Maybe Jesse was sorry already and was going to tell him it was all right.

Jesse grabbed him by the arm and his fingers dug in.

Jesse said, "I told you to beat it. Don't hang around here. Hit the road."

The fingers dug in even harder. Sammy wriggled from the pain. "But Jesse, where—"

Jesse pointed with the hand he wasn't using to hurt Sammy's arm. "There's tracks that way. Hit 'em and keep going. Tonight. If I find you round here tomorrow—"

Jesse didn't say what he'd do if he found Sammy around tomorrow. He just let go and walked away.

Far off in the night, in the direction in which Jesse had pointed, a freight engine whistled mournfully. The road, the hungry road. The road that had been before Jesse and the carnival. Hunger and freight cars clacking through the night, and running from brakemen and policemen, hiding and shivering in the cold.

But then a more cheerful thought came to him. Mr. Magus had told him he was going to have a lot of money, folding money, and soon. That must mean that the road was going to be different this time. Mr. Magus knew everything that was going to happen and Mr. Magus wouldn't tell him something that wasn't true.

And Sammy remembered now that the rules were different on the road. One rule was different, anyway. You could ask people for money or for food or for a chance to earn some of either. That is, you could ask at houses for food or money or a chance to work for some. Other hoboes you could ask just for food if they had some and you didn't. But the hoboes were more likely to share food with you than people in houses were likely to give you anything. At least it wasn't like here where you had to wait for somebody to ask you to run an errand. You seldom got enough food and you almost never got any money but at least you could ask.

And maybe this time if he asked people for money they'd give it to him, a lot of it, maybe that was what Mr. Magus had meant.

He started toward the side of the lot that was in the direction of the railroad tracks. The first thing was to get off the lot, now, tonight. He couldn't take a chance of Jesse seeing him in the morning. He'd have to walk until he came to the tracks and then walk and walk until he found a jungle, a freight yard. Tomorrow after it got light he could go to houses and start asking, but he'd have to walk hungry all night first.

He found himself cutting back off the midway between the freak show and the grab joint and stopped because he remembered that if he went that way he'd have to go past Mr. Evans's trailer.

But why shouldn't he go past it? Mr. Evans wouldn't come out and hit him just for walking past. Anyway, he could run, and he thought he could run faster than Mr. Evans. So why should he be afraid of him?

It came to him suddenly that he wasn't, any more. Why, if he had a tent stake or something he could even hit Mr. Evans if Mr. Evans tried to hurt him. And he hated Mr. Evans enough to hit him if Mr. Evans came after him. It was all right to hit to protect yourself. Except with Jesse.

He'd been moving forward slowly, now he could see the trailer and the lights were out. Mr. Evans was probably playing poker in the G-top. And if he was— Sammy's mouth began to water as he remembered that Mr. Evans had a little refrigerator in the trailer and kept food there; sometimes he made a meal for himself instead of going to the chow top. Food. The all-night walk ahead of him would be easy if he could fill his stomach first. And maybe there'd even be enough so that he could carry some with him and he could eat in the morning too.

But what if Mr. Evans was in there, in the dark? If he had a tent stake—but he didn't have one. They were all around him but they were all firmly driven into the ground and he couldn't pull one out all by himself.

Well, he could knock and if no one answered, he'd know Mr. Evans wasn't there. If Mr. Evans came to the door, he could just run.

He knocked and waited and knocked again louder and there wasn't any answer.

He tried the door and it was locked. But now he knew that no one was inside and with the pain in his stomach and the thought of food so near he wasn't going to let a looked door stop him. It would serve Mr. Evans right to have his door broken. He threw his shoulder against the door, and then again harder, and again. The third time did it but it made a loud noise, so instead of going in he ran around the outside of the trailer, around behind it and hid there, watching under it to see if anyone had heard the noise and was coming. No one came.

He walked around front again, on tiptoe. He went inside and turned on the lights. The door, with the lock broken, wouldn't stay shut until he thought of putting a chair against it.

Almost the first thing he saw as he turned toward the little refrigerator was a knife, an ordinary kitchen knife with an eight-inch blade, lying on the sink. That would be better than a tent stake, Sammy thought, if Mr. Evans came back while he was here. Much better. He wouldn't actually cut Mr. Evans with it unless Mr. Evans tried to hurt him—and Mr. Evans wouldn't dare try if he had that knife. He put it through his belt, handle upward so he could grab it quickly if he should need it.

Then he opened the refrigerator. It was disappointing. There was nothing in it but a little piece of butter in waxed paper, a little waxed cardboard carton that probably held cream, and some cans of beer. He picked up the cream and drank it; there was only a mouthful but it tasted wonderful. It was the first time he had ever tasted cream just by itself.

He opened the compartment over the refrigerator. His luck was better there. Half a box of marshmallow cookies; he stuffed one into his mouth right away. And an almost full box of crackers and the heel of a loaf of bread.

He'd eat the cookies here, fast, he decided. They'd be enough to stay that awful gnawing in his stomach. The other stuff, the crackers and the bread and the butter, he'd take along and stop somewhere to eat them a safe distance away, after he'd come to the tracks and walked along them for a while. There was a towel, a nice big one, over the sink. He could use it to make a bindle to carry the other food. He spread it out and put the crackers and the bread on it, then the butter. Still wolfing down cookies, he looked around for anything else that was eatable. He found a little jar of peanut butter and that was all. He put it with the rest and started making a bindle, out of the towel, and then stopped.

Why shouldn't he take along that book that had the interesting pictures in it? All of the books would be too heavy to carry with him and anyway some of them just had printing, but that one book wouldn't make his bindle too heavy and then tomorrow he could look at it as much as he wanted to. Even tonight if he came to a place along the tracks where there was enough light.

He popped another cookie into his mouth and opened the door of the compartment where the books had been.

It was empty.

Mr. Evans must have put the books somewhere else. Well, he'd find them, and while he was looking he might even find something else worth taking, some money; maybe. As long as he was stealing from Mr. Evans he might as well take anything else valuable— and easy to carry—that he could find. It would serve Mr. Evans right because it was Mr. Evans's fault that he was leaving the carnival tonight, Mr. Evans's fault he had to hit the road.

He opened other compartment doors and then drawers. He found quite a few little things that he put on the towel that was going to be his bindle. Things he might be able to sell or trade to somebody for food. He found a cigarette lighter, a necktie pin that had a big clear stone in it that must be a diamond, and a wrist watch that looked old and beat up but might still be worth something.

But not the books. He couldn't find the books. He still hadn't found them as he put the last marshmallow cookie into his mouth. He stood in the middle of the trailer looking around for doors or drawers that he hadn't opened. He thought to bend down and look under the bunk.

There was a suitcase under the bunk and he pulled it out. Maybe that was where Mr. Evans hid the books.

The suitcase was locked but he'd seen a hammer in a drawer a few minutes before so he got the hammer and hit the lock of the suitcase until it burst open.

It was nice swinging the hammer and it served Mr. Evans right to break the lock on his suitcase. For a moment he thought of using the hammer, now that it was in his hand, on other things in the trailer. Dishes, windows, everything that would break. But that would make too much noise. Someone would be sure to hear it and come. He tossed the hammer down on the bunk and lifted the lid of the suitcase.

On top, the first thing he saw, was a gun, a revolver. He picked it up and it felt nice and heavy in his hand. And deadly and dangerous. Holding it, he felt as though he was growing, bigger and stronger and more grown-up. Why, with this gun he wouldn't have to be afraid of anybody, ever. Not even Jesse. Even Jesse would be afraid of him with this gun. He didn't need the knife now; he took it out of his belt and tossed it on the bunk beside the hammer. He put the revolver into his side trousers pocket.

He looked down to see what else might be in the suitcase. He tossed out some neatly folded clothes.

There was a knock on the door, sharp and loud in the stillness of the night.

Sammy whirled and took the gun out of his pocket, pointing it at the door, his finger on the trigger, his thumb on the hammer ready to pull it back and cock it if the door started to open. But he wouldn't cock it unless the door opened because cocking a gun made it click and whoever was outside might hear. Sammy knew how to fire a revolver all right because once Mr. Weschenberg who ran the shooting gallery had asked him to do an errand and then had let him take a few shots with a rifle and a few with a revolver. He hadn't hit anything except one clay duck that he hadn't been aiming at, but he'd shot all right. And Mr. Weschenberg had showed him how, with a revolver, you pull back the hammer and cock it first and then pull the trigger when you're ready to shoot.

Now Sammy stood there, tense, quiet, waiting to see whether whoever had knocked was going to come on in.

He was so quiet that he scarcely breathed.

But not afraid.

CHAPTER TWENTY-FOUR

Just twenty minutes before, from the point of vantage he had taken for the purpose of watching, Dr. Magus had sighed with relief as he'd seen Barney King drive off the lot in his jalopy. And right after that he'd looked in the G-top and had seen that Burt was there, just buying chips to sit in the game. Nice to be sure Burt was occupied too, although the chance was negligible that he would have any reason to go back to his unborn show after it had closed for the night.

Now, back in the mitt camp and sitting in the dark so nobody would know he was there and drop in to chew the fat. Dr. Magus looked again at the luminous hands of his wrist watch and decided he'd given Barney enough time. If Barney had for any reason made a false start, had forgotten something and decided to come back for it, he'd have been back before this; by now he'd be too far on the road to come back and still meet that first plane.

His song and dance for Barney had been an easy one and well worked out. Of course luck had been a factor—Barney's bad luck at poker last night that had made ten bucks look big to him. If Barney had won heavily last night instead, he might have wanted to play again or might have had other plans, and even the twenty bucks Dr. Magus was prepared to raise his offer to might not have looked big enough to tempt him. And more than twenty he couldn't have offered; it would have looked out of line and therefore suspicious.

Yes, Dr. Magus thought, his luck had been in, all down the line since he'd got his first hunch. What a break he'd got at Glenrock—that wonderful head nurse remembering what Mack Irby had raved about while coming out from under the Sodium Pentothal. Of course he could give himself credit for having tossed her a beautiful con, a song and dance that had let him ask questions down the line, even about ravings under anesthetic; and his mention of forty-two toy soldiers had been a master stroke; it had given her a key to remembering. Forty-two G's, and then the hiding place handed to him on a silver platter. He'd hoped to get a lead, but not that he would get the big answer in one fell swoop.

The cardboard carton was ready, the rope inside it. He put it out under the canvas behind the mitt camp, in the shadows there. Now the final check-up. Barney's car still gone. Burt still in the poker game.

He got the carton from behind the mitt camp. He took it around behind the unborn show top. It was dark inside but he made sure by calling out Barney's name as he went under the canvas. He played his flashlight around thoroughly to make sure no drunken rideboy had crawled in here to sleep. Everything was okay. The top was empty except for things that belonged there. Including the jar with the forty-two thousand dollar calf fetus.

He reached under the canvas at the back and brought in the carton, The flashlight, lying on the ground, gave him enough light to put the jar into the carton and rope it shut. The jar was heavier than he'd guessed it would be; he was glad he'd be able to carry it by the rope.

Outside again, he stood for long seconds in the darkness, making sure that no one was near, no one was coming. Then he started around behind the tops again. He had a song and dance ready for anyone he might meet who might ask him what the hell he was carrying that looked so heavy, but he didn't meet anyone. He was almost sorry because the song and dance had been a good one and it was a shame to waste it.

In the mitt camp he unroped the carton and lifted the jar out of it, in darkness. No use risking even dim light until he needed it for the finer work of cutting the rubber. He tried the lid. It was a big lid, almost as big in diameter as the jar, and it was on tightly. He had to sit down with his legs wrapped around the jar and use both hands on the lid, one on each side. It turned, finally.

No smell of formaldehyde, the one thing he'd been afraid of.

It was in the bag. It was a lead pipe cinch. It was every other cliché he could think of. God still loved him and he could do no wrong.

And over two hours he had. Much more time than he needed, plenty of time to sigh happily and relax long enough to have a leisurely drink to fortify himself. Very carefully he hadn't taken a drink all day today, and now he deserved one, just one but a big one. It was going to be painstaking work cementing the rubber back again so the slit wouldn't show and no water would leak in. One big drink would make his hands steadier.

Still in darkness he found the bottle and a tumbler. This drink wasn't going to be straight from the bottle; he wanted to sip it, to savor and enjoy every drop of it. He used the flashlight briefly to see to the pouring. The glass was a six-ounce tumbler and he filled it half full of Old Bushmills. Bought for the purpose while he'd been in town that morning.

He raised the glass to his lips, sipped, and dreamed.

The money, the beautiful moolah, only inches and minutes away. Savor this moment, he told himself; realization will never equal it. This fleeting instant, this now, this anticipation—prolong it and enjoy it. Money will buy wonderful things but never a moment such as this one.

CHAPTER TWENTY-FIVE

After a while, after a long while, Sammy decided that whoever had knocked on the trailer door had gone away. He hadn't heard any footsteps, but then he hadn't heard any footsteps coming either. Whoever had been out there must have been wearing slippers or rubber soled shoes that made no sound on the grass. And he must have gone by now; he wouldn't still be standing there waiting this long after knocking. Sammy's muscles ached from the strain of standing so still. His arm ached from holding the revolver pointed at the door.

But he had to make sure that the knocker-on-the-door had really gone away before he went ahead with his searching. He kept the gun in his hand but put his hand around behind him out of sight and then went to the door. He moved the chair away and opened it. Nobody was in sight; he put his head out and looked all around to make sure.

He closed the door and put the chair against it again to hold it shut. He put the gun back in his pocket and returned to the suitcase. He threw out more clothes. The books didn't seem to be there. There were other things besides clothes, jars and bottles and three little boxes which he opened but whose contents didn't mean anything to him except that they didn't look valuable. And then he threw out the last of the clothes and at the bottom at one end of the suitcase was a shoe box.

He picked it up out of the suitcase—and took the lid off.

The shoe box was almost full of money, paper money, in neat stacks. Some of it in packages with paper bands around them, some of it loose.

Sammy stared at the money unbelievingly. He hadn't thought there was that much money in the whole world.

It was an awful lot of money. It must be enough money to buy anything. It must be a million dollars, or maybe a million million dollars. And Jesse had once told him that people who had a million dollars lived in big houses and had people to wait on them and everything they wanted. People who had a million dollars were rich.

Mr. Magus had been right! Sammy was rich already. Rich with paper money, folding money.

Bright pictures came to Sammy. All the cotton candy he could eat. Even a cotton candy machine of his own, like Mr. Magus had suggested, only he wouldn't want to hire someone to run it for him; why, pouring the pink sugar into it and watching the cotton candy form from it would be almost as much fun as eating it.

Now he could buy anything he wanted. He wouldn't want or need the bindle he'd started to make. He wouldn't have to eat those crackers; he could buy hamburger steaks any time he got hungry. Not tonight, maybe it would be too late to find a place open tonight, but his stomach was full at the moment from all the cookies he'd eaten.

Yes, he could forget the bindle. He had all he needed, the box of money and a gun to scare off anybody who tried to take it away from him. He wouldn't give this box of money even to Jesse, even if Jesse begged him to and wanted to take him back. This money was security, too, bigger and better security than he'd had with Jesse.

And in particular he'd never give it back to Mr. Evans. It served Mr. Evans right to have it taken away from him. Only he'd better leave quickly now before Mr. Evans came back because if he tried to take the money away from Sammy, Sammy would have to shoot him. And he didn't really want to shoot anybody, not even Mr. Evans, if he didn't have to. Because if he shot anybody the cops would come after him and they might catch him and put him in jail; then he couldn't spend the money.

He tiptoed to the door and looked around; there was nobody in sight so he stepped outside. He remembered then that he still hadn't found the book, the book with the pictures of naked men and women.

Almost he turned back, but then came the dizzying thought that with all that folding money he didn't need the book. He didn't have to look at pictures. Both Mr. King and Mr. Magus had told him that Miss Trixie would do those things with him if he gave her paper money.

Maybe even, now that he had a million million dollars, Miss Trixie would run away with him. And they could ride in taxicabs and on trains instead of hitting the road. They could stay in hotels and fancy places, and he'd buy lots of pretty things for Miss Trixie.

He had to find her now, right away.

He started toward the midway. He was so excited now that he didn't care if he ran into Jesse, or even if he ran into Mr. Evans and Mr. Evans recognized the box under his arm. If Mr. Evans asked for it back Sammy would just laugh at him and point the gun at him and Mr. Evans would run away.

Money and the gun gave Sammy a sense of power he'd never felt before. Something new, very heady. He felt as strong and as smart as anybody he might run into—and he had the gun besides. Its weight in his pocket felt good.

Gripping the shoe box tightly under his arm, he hurried toward the model show top to look for Miss Trixie. She probably wouldn't be there, but wherever she was he'd find her.

CHAPTER TWENTY-SIX

Trixie Connor put the final touch on her lipstick, standing close to the full length mirror in the dressing room of the model show. She looked all right, she decided. Her face was a bit sharp, but it always had been; she couldn't do anything about that. She stepped back for a full length view of herself and pirouetted. The full length view was good. She was small but her body was perfect. She'd been called a "pocket Venus" more than once and she loved the phrase. Almost as well as she loved the body it described. Loved it and loved to show it. Posing was pure pleasure for Trixie. Her only beef with her job was the fact that in most towns the Law insisted upon at least nominal covering, a gauzy bra and a G-string. In places where the Law was tough, really Sunday School, and the girls had to wear opaque bras and wider G-strings, Trixie wasn't happy. But then again there were the few places where they could pose really naked—of course with a hand and a forearm held like September Morn held them (but she could always manage to drop her arm a little, as though accidentally, just as they started to draw the curtain)—and when the carney played in such places she was cheerful and happy. Of course she'd posed for artists too, and that was good in a way because she could pose completely naked and not have to pretend to be coy about it, but it wasn't good really because there was only one man looking at her and most of the time looking at her as something to paint and not something to want. Posing for art classes was a little better but not much. Carney posing was best because the marks all looked at her the way she wanted to be looked at, the way that gave her kicks.

The carney paid well, too, and that was important because next to herself Trixie loved money. Some day she was going to have a lot of money, big money, money enough to do anything she pleased—and she had some ideas about what that would be although they weren't as definite as the plan itself, the plan for getting the money.

The plan hadn't worked yet, but it would work soon, maybe this coming winter. It was so simple that it had to work sooner or later. All through the carnival season, for the three seasons now since she'd thought of the plan, Trixie had saved her money. Her outside money, that is. Since her pay for modeling was enough for her to live well and dress well, she saved every dollar she could make on the side, after hours, selling what all men wanted, carneys and marks alike. It wasn't something that she wanted to do but she didn't mind doing it; in fact, once in a while she mildly enjoyed it. For three seasons now she'd saved every dollar she'd made that way and it had always amounted enough to let her carry out the plan.

The plan meant spending the winter—or as much of it as her stake would allow—at a swanky Florida winter resort, a place to which only people who were filthy rich went. She picked a different place each year, but always a very expensive resort hotel with a patio swimming pool. The more it cost the better, even though her stake would last a shorter period. She spent her afternoons sunning herself and acquiring a golden tan beside the pool. (And mornings lying nude under a sun lamp in her room so the tan would be all over and wouldn't mar her body for posing.) Sooner or later, spending her winters like that, she'd catch herself a rich man who'd want her so badly that he'd marry her. She'd come close already, a dozen times. And God knows there'd been no lack of propositions short of marriage; plenty of them had wanted her for a mistress and she could have had her choice of penthouse apartments. But she wanted more than that—or, rather, less than that. She wanted to marry a rich man so she wouldn't have to live with him, not longer than a month or so, anyway; then she could get a divorce and a financial settlement and be independent. Like Tommy Manville's ex's. Someone like Tommy Manville she wanted. But nothing less than a marriage certificate to go with him; how could you divorce a man and hook him unless he married you first? And it was strictly her business if she was a chippy all summer so she could afford to be strictly virtuous all winter, or whatever part of all winter she could afford to spend among the rich. The two things evened out, didn't they? One paid for and complemented the other and she enjoyed both lives. Someday the combination would pay off, someday she'd hit the jackpot.

She looked at her watch. Ten minutes after one, ten minutes late for her date. But the mark would wait that long; he'd probably wait half an hour or an hour before he decided she wasn't coming. If he didn't want her badly enough to do that, he wouldn't be good for the kind of dough she expected to take him for anyway so he wouldn't be much of a loss. It was good for a man to be kept waiting and wondering at least for a little while.

She put the lipstick back in her purse and, seeing the note there, took it out and read it again. It had been in an envelope that had also held a ten-dollar bill. The mark had given the envelope to the ticket taker, and had probably handed him a buck to deliver it to her. She got notes from marks a dozen or more times a week—all three of the girls did. Nine out of ten of them she just tore up but once in a while one looked as though the mark would put cash on the line and had enough of it to interest her, so she followed through. This one had definitely interested her because of that ten-dollar bill.

The note—she read it again now—read: "Dear Trixie Connor—(he knew her name, of course because the Poses and the poser were announced each time just before the curtain was pulled. 'Miss Trixie Connor as Queen of the Roses'; that was the pose in which she wore four roses—one was in her hair, if you're curious.) This is my calling card. There are a few more like it if you would like to meet me tonight after the show. I don't know how late it runs but one o'clock ought to be safe. At one o'clock I'll be parked on Beech Street just around the corner from the carnival lot, in a light blue Buick coupe. Please come, honey. You won't be sorry."

He'd be a live one all right if he'd been willing to gamble a sawbuck just to get her attention and without knowing whether she ever put out for money or not. A few times she'd had five-dollar bills in notes the same way, and had done all right with the guys who'd sent them, but this was the first time anyone had enclosed a ten. She could count on at least another fifty out of him and maybe a hundred, especially if he wanted her to stay with him all night. A hundred bucks would be a nice addition to her winter fund. It was more than she could make in a week of sleeping around with carneys on the lot. Carneys aren't suckers; five bucks was par and twenty was just about the top she could ever get from one and that only for an all night stand.

She shoved the note back into her purse and took a final look in the big mirror before she turned off the light and left, stepping carefully under the canvas so it wouldn't muss her hair. She'd better hurry now; it was almost one-fifteen and he might decide fifteen minutes was long enough and that his ten bucks had been a bad investment.

She hurried between the tops, past the bally platform and out onto the midway, out into the light.

A voice called her name and she stopped and turned. It was only Sammy, poor halfwitted Sammy, coming toward her, almost running. He had a shoe box under his left arm and his face looked—different.

"Miss Trixie! I was just coming for you. I want—"

She spoke rapidly. "Sammy, I can't talk to you now. I'm late for a date." She turned and started walking again.

But Sammy was walking alongside her, walking as rapidly as she was. He opened the shoe box even as she turned to him to tell him to go away and not to follow her; he reached in and held out in front of her a handful of—

They were right under a light bulb. She could see it plainly and she couldn't be wrong. It was a handful of money—a handful of twenty and fifty-dollar bills!

Trixie Connor stopped as though she had walked into a stone wall.

Almost by reflex action her hand darted out and grabbed that handful of bills—Sammy's fingers released them without struggle. The quickest glance showed her it was real money, not stage money or queer; the bills were all well worn and they looked right and felt right.

She forgot all about the light blue Buick coupe.

She quickly unsnapped her purse and stuffed the money into it as she whirled to face Sammy.

"Sammy, where did you get that money?"

He grinned at her. "I found it, Miss Trixie."

"Let me see that box!" She clutched at it but Sammy held onto it firmly; he was stronger than she.

He said quietly, "I'll let you see, Miss Trixie." As she let go he took off the lid and let her look. The light bulb overhead threw light into the box. Trixie gasped. Hundreds and hundreds of bills were stacked in there. Big denomination bills, most of them. At a quick glance it looked like maybe a hundred thousand dollars, maybe half a million.

Her mind clicked into overdrive. She did what she should have done seconds ago; she looked around quickly to see if anyone was watching them. No one was, and that meant for sure that nobody else knew Sammy had that money. They'd be sticking close to Sammy and planning to get it away from him. As she was right now.

It didn't matter where the money came from. Nothing mattered but how to get it for herself.

She put her hand on his arm and pulled him out from under that glaring and dangerous light, back into the shadows between the tops. Sammy pulled willingly.

Nothing like trying the simplest thing first. She put her arms around his neck and pressed herself against him. "Sammy, do you want to go to bed with me?"

"Gee, sure, Miss Trixie. That's what I give you the money for. It's enough, ain't it, what I give you?"

She could have said no and got another handful, but it was more important not to make him suspicious or even to let him wonder if she was greedy. She said, "Sure, Sammy, that was enough. For that much you can spend all night with me. And let's go to a hotel downtown."

"Whatever you say, Miss Trixie."

"Now listen to me, Sammy. You keep that box closed, don't let anybody else see inside it. Understand, Sammy? And let me do the talking, all the talking—to the taxi driver, to the hotel clerk, to anybody we have to talk to. And let me pay for things so you won't have to open the box. We can straighten that out later between us. Do you understand, Sammy?"

"Sure, Miss Trixie. Gee, I never stayed at a hotel before, so you know what to do and I don't. You mean we're going to take a taxi? I never took no taxi before either."

"That's why you should let me handle everything, honey. Yes, we'll take a taxi if one goes by and we can hail it. If one doesn't we'll walk; it's only about twenty blocks to town. We can walk twenty blocks, can't we, honey?"

"Gee, sure, Miss Trixie."

"But now listen and let me explain some things before we start so you won't make any mistakes. We want to do this so we won't take any chances of a hotel detective walking in on us, anything like that to spoil things. I've got a couple of suitcases and we'll take them; we'll go back and get them first thing. And at the hotel we'll register—I mean I'll register for both of us, as brother and sister, and we'll ask for separate rooms."

Her mind was working furiously now, trying to figure all the angles at once, anything that could go wrong. Brother and sister it had to be and for separate rooms. No hotel clerk would swallow their registering as husband and wife.

"Sammy, can you pretend you're deaf and dumb?"

"How, Miss Trixie?"

"Just don't talk, don't talk at all, while we're in the taxi or registering in the hotel. Just let me do everything."

She was pulling him by the arm now, walking fast, thinking fast, checking every angle. First the suitcases—and get the shoe box into one so nobody who might recognize it would see it. Thank God she had some sleeping tablets in one of the suitcases already and part of a bottle of whisky. At the hotel she'd give him a doctored drink so that once he slept he'd sleep long and soundly and by the time he woke she'd be hundreds of miles away, switching trains and planes and buses, making a trail that couldn't be followed. Because somebody—cops or robbers; it didn't matter which—would be coming after that money. But give her even a few hours start and they'd never catch her.

"Sammy, honey, come on, hurry."

CHAPTER TWENTY-SEVEN

The murderer held three aces and had opened. Jesse Rau and Al Ritchie had stayed. He masked his hand by holding a jack for a kicker and took one card. He put his one card with the others without looking at it because Jesse and Al were each taking one card too. He said, "Check it blind."

Neither of them had raised his opening bet so they were going, probably, for straights or flushes. They'd play him for two pair, waiting for a bet against him to see whether or not he'd filled; it would make them careful.

Jesse looked at his card and then counted out five dollar chips and put them in. Al hesitated, or pretended to hesitate, and then called.

He fanned his cards slowly. The three aces were still there—and the fourth one had joined them. Four beautiful aces, the winning hand.

He counted out five chips, pretended to hesitate, and then counted out five more.

Someone slid into the vacant seat behind him. He glanced over his shoulder and saw that it was Wiggins. He said, "Hi, Wiggy. Going to sit in?"

"For a while. Say, you left the light on in your trailer." He managed not to start, looking down to hide whatever fright might be showing in his eyes. He hadn't left the light on. He'd turned out the light and he'd locked the door. After his experience with Sammy walking in the other night, he never had left the trailer without being absolutely positive that the light was out and the door locked. And the money—

He asked, "How long ago? Just now?" He prayed that it was. He wanted to throw in his hand and run but he couldn't throw in, not just after raising.

Wiggins said, "It was fifteen or twenty minutes ago." Suddenly he was sweating. He couldn't sit it out, even if running off looked suspicious.

He jumped up as though remembering something. He shoved the cards into Wiggins's hand. "Play these for me, Wiggy. My God, I just remembered. I got the week's take in there, and I didn't leave the light on."

He broke into a run as soon as he was outside. He could see his trailer as soon as he'd taken a dozen steps; the light was still on and now the door was ajar. When he got there and went in he saw that the lock on the door was broken.

The suitcase on the floor. Empty . . . Even the clothes had been taken out and thrown on the bed. And the shoe box was gone. So was the gun.

Blankly he looked around. The food taken out of the refrigerator and cupboard—the empty box that had held cookies—Sammy.

Only Sammy would have broken in here to look for food, to have eaten cookies while he searched the trailer looking for something else to steal. Sammy on the lam; Jesse had said something about kicking Sammy out.

But he must have left after Wiggins had been here— the door being ajar was a much more conspicuous fact than the lights being on. If the door had been ajar when Wiggins had been by he'd have said so, not have said just that the lights were on. Sammy had still been in here then and had left since then, maybe only minutes ago. He might still be on the lot; he couldn't be far away.

The Murderer rushed out, not bothering to turn off the lights or to close the door. They didn't matter now and every second might count.

On the midway he stopped, looking around for someone, anyone, who might have seen Sammy, who might be able to tell him which way Sammy had gone.

He ran for the chow top, seeing that it was still lighted. In the entrance he almost ran into Dixie. "Seen Sammy?"

"You mean Rau's boy? Yeah, maybe five minutes ago."

"Where? Which way was he going?"

"Toward the main gate. He was with Trixie Connor, carrying a couple suitcases for her."

"They have a taxi waiting?"

Dixie shrugged. "I just saw 'em go by."

He gasped thanks and ran toward the gate. Then he whirled and ran for his car instead. Even if they'd had a cab waiting or had been lucky enough to flag one already, he might be able to catch them.

CHAPTER TWENTY-EIGHT

Dr. Magus shifted the shielded flashlight and looked again to be sure. Yes, the line was faint but unmistakable. It had been cleverly cut along the fold under the shoulder so it couldn't be seen through the glass of the . . .

He picked up the single-edged razor blade he had ready for the purpose and ran it lightly along the line, then a little harder. It was merely cemented shut with rubber cement such as he had ready to cement it shut with again.

The cut opened.

He dropped the razor blade and reached his fingers in eagerly through the cut.

He touched paper, the crisp wonderful paper of United States currency.

This was the moment. He sighed deeply with satisfaction, realizing now how tense he had been, realizing now that until this moment, despite all evidence, he had doubted that fate could be so kind to one so undeserving.

Puzzlingly, the bills seemed to be tied together and to be tied to something. He pulled.

There was a flash.

• • •

Weep no tears for Dr. Magus. He died the best of deaths. He died without even hearing the sound of the explosion that killed him, died so suddenly that there was no time for either pain or realization. He died without knowing that he died, and in a moment of supreme satisfaction and happiness. What more could he have asked or wanted?

CHAPTER TWENTY-NINE

Weep rather for Burt Evans, owner of the unborn show, the murderer now of five people if one counts Leon Quintana, and all for a shoe box full of money he no longer had.

Through the windshield of his car, as he stepped on its starter, he saw the flash, as Dr. Magus had, but he heard the explosion too. He saw the canvas of the mitt camp billow outward and tear.

In his travail he thought, Oh God, what now? Had that been the booby trap he'd put inside the rubber calf fetus, the booby trap that had been for Mack Irby in case Mack got back from the hospital unexpectedly and got to the fetus to take the money from it before he could get to Irby and kill him?

It must have been; it must be that Dr. Magus had somehow got on the trail of that money too and had learned where it was hidden. Rather, where it had been hidden before he'd found it and put it in the shoe box in his suitcase. But how could Doc have learned about it?

Well, that didn't matter now. Or . . . Oh God, yes it did. If that explosion had been the booby trap in the pickled punk, then it meant he couldn't come back to the lot now whether or not he caught up with Sammy and Trixie and the money. Because the police would find fragments of rubber and fragments of glass that would add up to a five-gallon jar and they'd find the two-headed calf fetus missing from the unborn show, and he'd have some impossible questions to answer.

And Sammy and Trixie were a danger even aside from the money because they'd never make a clean getaway with it. However it happened that the two of them got together on it, they'd never get away with it. They weren't smart enough. Even Trixie wasn't smart enough if she ditched Sammy on the deal as she probably planned to. They'd get Sammy anyway. And Sammy would tell where he'd found the money and that would be that. The police would put it all together, finally, the booby-trapped punk, the murder of Mack Irby, the bank robbery just before the accident, the whole damn thing. They might never even suspect him of having engineered Dolly's death and Linder's, and they'd have a hell of a time now pinning Mack Irby's murder on him. But they'd have him cold on Dr. Magus.

Win, lose or draw on catching up Sammy and Trixie, he had to keep on going now. And unless he got the money back, he'd have lost everything. His show, his own money—in the bank but he'd never dare show up to try to draw it out—his trailer, even his clothes except the ones he was wearing. Every second counted; he couldn't go back to the trailer, even for his razor or an extra shirt. Most of the money that had been in his pocket was invested in chips in that damn poker game.

The engine was running now. He jerked the car viciously into gear and turned on the lights. He started off, circling to go off the other side of the lot, away from the excitement, from the rush of people heading toward what was left of the mitt camp.

He'd been so careful, so damned careful just so that he could spend the money openly, without having to go into hiding and take a new identity and worry about being hunted all his life. He'd planned to that end from the very moment when he'd found the money. That had been three days after the accident that had killed Flack and had put Irby in the hospital. He'd noticed that the water level had gone down several inches in the jar that held the two-headed calf fetus. He'd found the jar lid was tight so he'd known that the hollow rubber fetus—the only fake one in the lot—must have sprung a leak that was letting water seep into it from the jar. He'd taken it out to hunt for and fix the leak and he'd found the cut Irby had made and had imperfectly cemented shut.

And of course he'd looked inside and found the money; it had been soaking wet and it had been a hell of a job getting it dried out and still keeping it out of sight.

He'd guessed the score right off. Flack and Irby and a bank robbery. Checking a newspaper had confirmed it. And Flack was dead and Irby, the only person who knew about the money being there, in the hospital.

He'd had plenty of time to think things out and to get ready for Irby's return. He made the booby trap and set it. The minute he learned that Irby was back he'd watch for a chance to kill him without being caught. And if that worked, he figured, he could ride out the rest of the season, retire and enjoy life. But in case Irby made a try for the money first the booby trap would have taken care of him.

Of course in that case he'd have taken it on the lam with the money the minute he heard the explosion. Wherever he was on the lot—and he'd made a point of never leaving it when Irby's return became imminent— he'd have heard the bomb go off and all he had to do was put the suitcase in the car and drive away.

Where had he made a mistake? None, that he could see. How could he have forseen a halfwit searching his trailer for food and finding the money?

How could he have foreseen Dr. Magus springing the booby trap? Of course he could have taken the dynamite out any time since last Monday night, but it would have been more dangerous to dismantle the trap than it had been to make it and put it in the punk. He'd figured he might as well leave it there and after the end of the season bury the whole thing, jar and punk and booby trap all together, or maybe drop it off a bridge or into deep water from a boat.

Off the lot and onto the street. Shouts behind him, but they were not shouts at him.

He swung around the corner with tires screeching and then slowed down. If Trixie and Sammy were still waiting for a taxi or had started to walk, he didn't want to drive past without seeing them. If they were walking they couldn't have gone more than a few blocks; he'd have to drive slowly and watch carefully for a while and then go like hell to try to catch a cab if they'd got one. Luckily he didn't have to worry about what route they'd take; this street was a main drag leading right into the heart of town.

He drove two blocks slowly and he hadn't passed them. And for the next two blocks ahead there weren't any trees along the sidewalk; he could speed up and still not miss them. Damn them, they must have caught a cab.

He hit the floorboards with the accelerator pedal. The needle climbed to sixty and kept on climbing. His mind was going as fast as the car, figuring what he could do if he reached downtown without having caught up to them.

Check railway depot and bus depot first. Phone the airport from one of them, if there was an airport. Then start checking hotels. He thought it would be a hotel— although of course the depots came first because if it was a hotel there wasn't any hurry. He felt almost sure it would be a hotel because Trixie would want to ditch Sammy and a hotel would give her a chance. They wouldn't register under their own names but God knows they'd be an easy enough couple to describe.

There was a car ahead that looked as though it could be a taxi. He didn't slow down; he swung out to go around it and as he pulled level he looked across into it. It was a squad car. Two startled faces under uniform caps looking at him. "Pull over!"

He held his foot down and went on past them almost as though they were standing still. Behind him their siren started to wail as they gathered speed for the chase. But his momentum gave him a full block lead. Could he get away from them? He had to now. If he'd stopped right away they might only have given him a ticket but now they'd pull him in for sure. Hell, they would have pulled him in anyway, even if he'd stopped when they'd yelled to him to pull over. He'd been going over eighty, in town, and his car had an out of state license.

A red stop light ahead. To hell with that. He kept his foot down. But a car came out from the cross street; he had to swing the wheel hard to miss it. He missed it, but he'd swung too sharply. The world tilted, turned upside down, and ended in a scream of tearing metal.

CHAPTER THIRTY

Sammy put down the suitcases. Behind him he heard Miss Trixie slide home the bolt of the door. He turned. She looked eager, excited. Her eyes were shining. He felt eager and excited himself now. He'd heard people talk about being in love and had never known what it meant until just now. The way he felt now, that was being in love. He loved Trixie.

He took a step toward her, but she smiled and put up a hand to hold him off. "Honey, don't rush me. I want to get my breath. And we got all night, honey."

"Sure, Miss Trixie."

She walked around him and opened one of the suitcases. It was the one that had been empty; they'd put the shoe box in it and a bottle Miss Trixie had had and then she'd tossed enough clothes in to fill it.

Sammy thought maybe she was going to reach for the box of money and that was his so he moved over to stop her if she did, but she reached only for the bottle.

"Sammy, I'll make us each a drink." She looked at him thoughtfully for a second. "Here's what let's do. I think you ought to take a bath before we go to bed. Will you do that, honey?"

"Sure, Miss Trixie."

"And while you're doing that, I'll make us each a nice drink and I'll get undressed and be in bed waiting for you and the drinks will be ready too."

"Sure, Miss Trixie."

"And close the bathroom door, will you, honey? The sound of water running always gives me the jim-jams."

"All right, Miss Trixie."

Sammy started for the bathroom and then turned back. "Now, Miss Trixie, you wouldn't run off with that money, would you? That's my money, and I don't want you to run off with it."

She laughed heartily. "Word of honor as a girl scout. When you come out all nice and clean I'll be here and the money will be here and I'll be waiting for you."

Sammy went into the bathroom and shut the door. He put the plug in the bathtub and started the water running. But he was still a little worried about the money. He loved Miss Trixie and he believed her, but what if he was wrong in believing her? That must be an awful lot of money in the box; he remembered the look on Miss Trixie's face when she'd looked into the box.

He happened to look up and saw that there was a transom above the bathroom door. The glass in the transom was the wavy kind that you can't see through, but it was open a little; he'd be able to see through the crack at the bottom if he got up there.

But he wasn't tall enough to see through that crack, and there wasn't any way of climbing up there. He looked down to see if the bathroom door had a keyhole he could look through, but it didn't have. There was a knob that probably locked it but there wasn't any keyhole.

He turned back to see if the water was running warm enough and that was when he saw the stool. It was a stool to sit on, but it suddenly came to Sammy that he could stand on it too, and that if he moved it over by the door and stood on it there, he could see through the bottom of the transom. And then he could see what Miss Trixie was doing out there and she wouldn't know that he was seeing. He moved the stool over in front of the door and stepped up onto it.

If Miss Trixie started to undress and get into bed, then he'd know for sure that she wasn't going to run away with the money while he was taking a bath. And anyway it would be nice to watch her undress and get naked.

But Miss Trixie wasn't running off with the money nor was she getting undressed yet; she was making the drinks. She'd already poured whisky, about three fingers of it, into each of the two tumblers on the bureau. Now she had a little box and she took some little white things, about six or seven of them, out of the box and put them into one of the glasses and started to stir it with a fingernail file she took out of the purse that was still hanging from her arm. She must be making something fancy for them to drink, not just plain whisky. Sammy knew that people mixed things to make fancy drinks.

He was getting hot from the steam that was coming up from the water running in the tub. There'd been two faucets and he'd known one of them must be hot and the other cold but he hadn't known which and had turned one at random. It had been the hot water, he knew now. So he got down from the stool and turned it off and turned the other one on. Then he got on the stool.

Miss Trixie still hadn't started to undress. But she'd finished mixing the drinks and she was kneeling in front of the suitcase, the one that was open and had the shoe box in it, and she moved the clothes until the shoe box showed. She picked up the shoe box and took the lid off, standing up now and looking in and reaching in, moving some of the bills around.

She shouldn't do that. It was his money and not hers, and if she looked at it and touched it like that she might change her mind about running away with it.

Maybe it would be a good idea to scare her so she wouldn't do that. He remembered the gun in his pocket. Maybe he should scare her with it and let her know he had a gun so she'd be afraid to try to run away with his money.

He took the gun out of his pocket as he stepped down off the stool. He pulled back the hammer with his thumb—because the click it made wouldn't be heard over the roar of the running water now anyway—like the man at the shooting gallery had showed him how to do.

He opened the door and stepped out.

Miss Trixie jumped up, and from the look on her face he knew that he was scaring her all right. She backed away from him. She dropped the box of money and the money came out of the box and made a pile of money on the floor, a pile of green and white paper money.

And she took another step back and he decided he didn't want to scare her too much. He loved her and he didn't want her to look at him like that.

He said, "I ain't going to hurt you, Miss Trixie. I just want to show you that I—"

The gun went off in his hand.

Why, his finger had just been resting on the trigger; it hadn't been pulling hard like he'd had to pull on the trigger of the revolver at the shooting gallery!

The noise it made was awful in that little room.

But the look on Miss Trixie's face was even more awful. And suddenly her head and shoulders bent forward and she fell down on the floor. She jerked and rolled over, her head toward him.

Sammy let go of the gun and it fell on the floor too. He said, "I'm sorry, Miss Trixie, I didn't mean—"

She didn't move or answer. But maybe he hadn't really shot her. Maybe the noise had just scared her and she'd fainted.

Sammy got down on the floor by her and put her head in his lap. He saw now that there was a spreading red spot on her pretty green dress right between her breasts. And suddenly blood, a lot of blood, came out of her mouth; Sammy whimpered.

Her face wasn't pretty any more and Sammy looked away from it. He saw Miss Trixie's purse where it had fallen and spilled its contents. The handful of bills he had given her had come out of it and they were lying right next to the bills that had come out of the shoe box. And a book of matches had come out of her purse and was lying there too.

There was hammering on the door of the room and yelling outside in the corridor and somebody trying the knob and somebody yelling to somebody else to call the police, and Sammy was staring at the pile of money and the book of matches and thinking that now Mr. Evans would get the money back, and Sammy reaching for the matches and striking one and touching it to the money, and flames going up as the money started to burn, and Sammy moving more and more of the five and ten and twenty and fifty and hundred dollar bills onto the fire and Miss Trixie's eyes glazing over and more hammering on the door and yelling and the roar of water still running in the bathroom and the flames getting higher and higher and prettier and prettier and hotter and hotter and brighter and brighter.

THE END

FREDRIC BROWN BIBLIOGRAPHY
(1906-1972)

MYSTERIES:

Ed and Am Hunter series
The Fabulous Clipjoint (1947)
The Dead Ringer (1948)
The Bloody Moonlight (1949; UK as Murder in the
   Moonlight, 1950)
Compliments of a Fiend (1950)
Death Has Many Doors (1951)
The Late Lamented (1959)
Mrs. Murphy's Underpants (1963)

Murder Can Be Fun (1948; reprinted as A Plot for
   Murder, 1949)
The Screaming Mimi (1949)
Here Comes a Candle (1950)
Night of the Jabberwock (1950)
The Case of the Dancing Sandwiches (1951)
The Far Cry (1951)
We All Killed Grandma 1952)
The Deep End (1952)
Madball (1953)
His Name Was Death 1954)
The Wench is Dead (1955)
The Lenient Beast (1956)
The Office (1958; mainstream)
One for the Road (1958)
Knock Three-One-Two (1959)
The Murderers (1961)
The Five Day Nightmare (1962)
Homicide Sanitarium (1984; stories)
Before She Kills (1984; stories)
The Freak Show Murders (1987; stories)
Thirty Corpses Every Thursday (1987; stories)
Pardon My Ghoulish Laughter (1987; stories)
Red Is the Hue of Hell (1990; stories)

SCIENCE FICTION:

Mitkey Astromouse (1941; children's story, reprinted
    1971)
Space on My Hands (1951; stories)
What Mad Universe (1951)
Project Jupiter (1953; reprinted as The Lights in the
    Sky are Stars, 1954)
Angels and Spaceships (1954; stories, reprinted as Star
    Shine, 1956)
Martians, Go Home (1955)
Rogue in Space (1957)
Honeymoon in Hell (1958)
The Mind Thing (1961)
Nightmares and Geezenstacks (1961; stories)
Daymares (1968; stories)
Paradox Lost (1973; stories)
The Best of Fredric Brown (1977; stories)
The Best Short Stories of Fredric Brown (1982; stories)
And the Gods Laughed (1985; stories)
From These Ashes (1985; stories)
Daymare and Other Tales from the Pulps (2007;
    stories)
Earthmen Bearing Gifts (2010; with A Prize for Edie by
    J. F. Bone)

EDITOR:

Science Fiction Carnival (1953; co-edited with Mack
    Reynolds)

BIOGRAPHY OF FREDRIC BROWN:

Martians and Misplaced Clues: The Life and Work of

Fredric Brown was born on October 29, 1906 in Cincinnati, Ohio. According to his wife, Brown hated to write. So he did everything he could to avoid it—he'd play his flute, challenge a friend to chess, or tease his cat. But when he did write, he produced work in a wide variety of genres: mystery, science fiction, black comedy, sometimes all in the same work. His first science fiction story, "Not Yet the End," was published in 1941, and one of his stories, "Arena," was adapted as an episode of *Star Trek*. *The Fabulous Clipjoint*, Brown's first mystery novel, won the Edgar Award for outstanding first mystery and began a series featuring Ed and Ambrose Hunter, carny-relatives turned detectives. Brown was a newspaperman by trade, married twice with two sons, who devoted all-to-little of his life to fulltime writing. He died on March 11, 1972 in Tucson at age 65 from emphysema.

Black Gat Books

Black Gat Books is a new line of mass market paperbacks introduced in 2015 by Stark House Press. New titles appear every three months, featuring the best in crime fiction reprints. Each book is sized to 4.25" x 7", just like they used to be. Collect them all

1 Haven for the Damned
by Harry Whittington
978-1-933586-75-5, $9.99

2 Eddie's World
by Charlie Stella
978-1-933586-76-2, $9.99

3 Stranger at Home
by Leigh Brackett writing as
George Sanders
978-1-933586-78-6, $9.99

4 The Persian Cat
by John Flagg
978-1933586-90-8, $9.99

5 Only the Wicked
by Gary Phillips
978-1-933586-93-9, $9.99

6 Felony Tank
by Malcolm Braly
978-1-933586-91-5, $9.99

7 The Girl on the Bestseller List
by Vin Packer
978-1-933586-98-4, $9.99

8 She Got What She Wanted
by Orrie Hitt
978-1-944520-04-5, $9.99

9 The Woman on the Roof
by Helen Nielsen
978-1-944520-13-7, $9.99

10 Angel's Flight
by Lou Cameron
978-1-944520-18-2, $9.99

11 The Affair of Lady Westcott's Lost Ruby /
The Case of the Unseen Assassin
by Gary Lovisi
978-1-944520-22-9, $9.99

12 The Last Notch
by Arnold Hano
978-1-944520-31-1, $9.99

13 Never Say No to a Killer
by Clifton Adams
978-1-944520-36-6, $9.99

14 The Men from the Boys
by Ed Lacy
978-1-944520-46-5 $9.99

15 Frenzy of Evil
by Henry Kane
978-1-944520-53-3 $9.99

16 You'll Get Yours
by William Ard
978-1-944520-54-0 $9.99

17 End of the Line
by Dolores & Bert Hitchens
978-1-944520-57 $9.99

18 Frantic
by Noël Calef
978-1-944520-66-3 $9.99

Stark House Press

1315 H Street, Eureka, CA 95501 707-498-3135
griffinskye3@sbcglobal.net   www.starkhousepress.com
Available from your local bookstore or direct from the publisher.

www.ingramcontent.com/pod-product-compliance
Lightning Source LLC
Chambersburg PA
CBHW070951180726
48291CB00004B/1241

"The man did it all! Hard-boiled mystery, paradoxical sf, short fantasy, black comedy-and sometimes, all of the above. That's what makes Brown's work so damned fun. He crossed genres like a demon, plotted like a madman, and continually stretched the boundaries of any given genre into his own strange, private geography."
—*Thrilling Detective* website

"*Madball* is a terrific pulp novel that is filled with energy and excitement from cover to cover... Brown fills this novel with all manner of thieves, murderers, strippers, carnival barkers, knife throwers, drifters, fortune tellers, and others... all linked together by stolen money, jealousy, fear, lust, and greed."
—Dave Wilde

"Perhaps his best mystery novel."
—Frank McSherry

"This novel is deliciously dark, suspenseful, slightly comedic and ribald... be sure not to miss this one—Mr. Brown will charm you and hold you in uneasy rapt attention."
—Michael Schramm

"*Madball* is a dark crime story set at a carnival and dealing with all the various characters that make the carnival work. From the stereotypical owner, Wiggins, to Dr. Magus, the mentalist, to the talkers and grinders and performers and other show people, we are introduced to the full array... a brilliant and entertaining tale."
—Ron Zack